THE MAN IN THE BUICK

AND OTHER STORIES

Whether she is writing about photographers, an artist, a writer, in stories set in upstate New York, Pittsburgh, Mexico, or China, Kathleen George deftly plays out themes of discordant love, sometimes resolved, and finds a lucid voice to let her characters come alive on the page. The grace of her writing, the intensity of her insights assert themselves in memory and won't let go.

—Colette Inez

Kathleen George is an assured and elegant writer and storyteller possessed of an exceptionally commodious embrace. One after another, these wise and moving accounts of essential human striving wrap themselves around whole lifetimes of love and hunger, memory and loss. Delightfully readable as these stories are, to enter them is to give oneself over to a delicate mortal struggle for understanding. George is not aiming to make things easy. Her devotions are to what is complex, what is hard won, what is *true*. She performs this austere practice with a singular grace, and each one of these stories falls into a reader's hands like a precious gift.

—Susan Dodd

I will read *The Man in the Buick* over and over again. I will teach it to my students. I will buy copies for my friends. I will recommend it to friendly strangers. I will do these things because of the uncommon honesty of these stories, their sharp, shimmering prose, and the characters in them, so palpable and deep thinking and interesting, so infuriating and wise, so funny and sad that I actually missed them when I closed the book. These kinds of stories are so rare in our world, you've got to keep them close at hand…and pass them on to those you care about as though you were giving them the secrets to a long and beautiful life.

—Reginald McKnight

THE MAN IN THE BUICK

AND OTHER STORIES

BY

KATHLEEN GEORGE

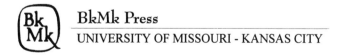

BkMk Press
UNIVERSITY OF MISSOURI - KANSAS CITY

MAC
MISSOURI ARTS COUNCIL

Financial assistance for this book has been provided by the Missouri
Arts Council, a state agency.

Cover design by Robert C. T. Steele

Library of Congress Cataloging-in-Publication Data

George, Kathleen
    The man in the buick and other stories / by Kathleen George.
        p.   cm.
    Contents: The tractor accident — María — The man in the buick —
    Chinese massage — Flight — Weeds — Small errands — Sighting —
    The elephant boy — Things progress.
        ISBN 1-886157-20-0
    1.   United States — Social life and customs — 20th century —
    Fiction.
    I.   Title. II. Title: Man in the Buick.
    PS3557.E487M36   1999
    813' .54 — dc21   99-19247
                                                             CIP

Grateful acknowledgment is made to the editors of the following publications in which these stories first appeared:

Alaska Quarterly Review	"Sighting"
American Fiction	"María"
Cimarron Review	"Things Progress"
Great Stream Review	"Flight"
Gulf Stream	"Weeds"
North American Review	"The Tractor Accident"
Other Voices	"Small Errands"
West Branch	"Chinese Massage" and "The Man in the Buick"

The author wishes to acknowledge the support of the MacDowell Colony, the University of Pittsburgh, the Virginia Center for the Creative Arts, and the Pennsylvania Council on the Arts.

For Hilary

CONTENTS

Whenever I take up a newspaper and read it, I fancy I see ghosts creeping between the lines. There must be ghosts all over the world. They must be as countless as the grains of the sands . . . .

—Henrik Ibsen, *Ghosts*

THE TRACTOR ACCIDENT

I

I've gathered the facts, memorized the details. Here is what happened.

Garren had been married to Nell for twenty-seven years and living on the farm in upstate New York for most of those. It was 1982. Their children were no longer around; they were in Chicago, Indiana, school.

The tractor he owned was an International Harvester, a high wheel Cub. It was really a wonderful machine for a place like that. It could shovel snow, grade roads, cut hay (for this it had a sickle bar). It also had a rotary mower for lawns, or you could attach a trailer to it to haul firewood. It could plow up snow, really dig. Garren had bought it mainly to cut field hay.

It was an old thing, over twenty years old, but it still chugged along. He originally bought it in 1959, a one-thousand dollar demonstrator, at a place that sold farm supplies. He thought, do we need this, can we afford it? He decided they did because local farmers charged a lot to mow wild grasses and brush, which their property had plenty of. Now he could do all that himself. Which meant that he didn't have much time to do what he loved, taking photographs, and that was a problem.

The tractor looked like a stripped car. It had big rear wheels, five feet high, which Garren kept filled with anti-freeze, heavier than air, for traction. A saddle seat made it a bit like riding a horse. The whole thing had no cab or body to speak of. It was all engine, seat, and wheels. The engine itself was almost exposed except for a slight hood. The front wheels were little. They were that solid rubber kind attached to axles so they could turn sharply. Sometimes Garren thought the machine looked like a beast or an oversized insect. Also, it looked naked.

The season at the time of the accident was late spring or early summer. Garren was just back from a long winter job photographing the city of Denver. He had met Denise and he was in love.

"Tell me about Denver," Nell had asked him on the phone.

He'd said, "The architecture is unbelievably dull, but I'm finding angles, I'm finding light that flatters it. Somehow I'm taking good photographs. The city officials are happy." He'd been on these jobs, back and forth from the farm, for nine years. He taught classes sometimes. Mostly he photographed cities and factories. But he was also amazingly good at people. Faces. He was good at what he loved. Cities. Bustle, activity. The arts. Busy people.

The farm he lived on with Nell was her idea, a way of living well and simply at the same time. Nell said, "You see this? Isn't this wonderful?" She was looking out over the field hay to the fields beyond. Garren knew it was supposed to bring them peace. But when they came together, they argued. She found his need to take pictures boring, foolish. She made fun of him. "Sure. Capture the barn in black and white at sunset. But paint it red in daylight sometime soon."

Garren would go off on a job, see how he wanted his life to be, then go back to the farm, get on his tractor and work in the fields while Nell puttered in the kitchen or on the back porch. He asked her to move with him to the city, but she said absolutely not.

Then in 1982 he went to Denver for four months and met Denise.

Denise broke him down. All his resolve to keep things together melted away.

It was an old story, but it felt brand new when it happened to him. She was enrolled in a photography workshop he gave in Denver. She slipped in and out of his vision, in and out of the dark room, in and out of the restaurant he frequented until he finally asked her, heart beating, to have dinner with him one night. "I wondered when you were going to get around to it," she said. "Life is only so long."

For a week, he just talked to her. But the talk. . . well, she'd led a murky life. At the end of a week, he knew she'd had a long-term affair with a step-uncle, a business man, who was a familiar in her mother's house. She thought her mother had suspected the affair all along. Denise smoked dope when she told him these stories back in his rooms. He'd get mesmerized by her smallness, her little cat's eyes, and her smooth, lovely skin so that he was cushioned, as if he'd smoked too, from her stories of ongoing cocaine connections, three abortions, and a fast, fast life. He had wanted city life. She was city.

His whole relationship with Denise shook his system. She would twine around him, only to get up abruptly and leave or say something outrageously funny. She was a good mimic and could imitate him and just about everybody in their photography workshop. He laughed uneasily. Did she see through everyone so unsentimentally?

In a foggy dream, he took in details about her, a small mole on her upper right thigh, her hair curlier at the neckline, the fact that she slept with a pistol under her pillow. A pistol! Somehow he got used to it. Oh, yes, I'd better not turn over too abruptly, he'd think, because of the gun under her pillow. Uh, well, he imagined saying if ever he had to explain the gun to a law officer, she has to protect herself; she's had some rough characters in her life. She was cocaine, of course. She burned into his nose. She made him feel free.

On top of that she turned out to be a very talented photographer, although her very first set of pictures in which somehow most faces were disguised enough by light or other means to be almost unrecognizable were all of pimps and whores. Not sentimentally shown either, but caught in interesting poses and moods, as if what they did was a job, just hard work. Garren asked in class, taken aback, how she had gotten their trust. She said she just knew them.

He thought, soon I'll go home, leave her here, let this friendship, whatever it is, drift.

When the photography students in his class were invited to a party at one of the upscale galleries, he watched her move fluidly in these sophisticated circles. She could hold her own in conversation with anyone. Men fell over their wine glasses toward her. Who was he to sniff at her interest in him?

By midwinter they began to see each other daily. Nothing seemed very real. And yet it continued and became real. When spring brought wafts of new growth in the air, scents of flowers and leaves and wet earth, he suddenly couldn't imagine leaving her. One day he opened his apartment door to Nell and his son Michael who had come to fetch him home. Did Nell suspect? She wanted to see Denver, she said. She wanted to see his show at the gallery.

He went and found a phone and called Denise, desperate, saying he would find a way to stay on in Denver or get back to Denver. She told him nonsense, pooh, go home, he was married.

When he first got back to the farm, Garren snuck out regularly to phone Denise. He would go out on the road, to an isolated pay phone, carrying a pocketful of change. Sometimes there was no answer, but usually Denise was home, sounding sad, thinking, reading, studying photography manuals, photographs, things that would make her better and better at taking pictures. He told her he was going to leave Nell.

She said he shouldn't.

He told her he was going to take a long, boring assignment in Miami because he could fly out to see her or fly her down to see him.

She said she might move to San Francisco.

He said he would fly to San Francisco.

She said she loved him but she didn't want him to break up his marriage. She said she hadn't much wanted to live before he found something worthwhile in her.

The tractor accident happened one day when it was still early summer. It was very warm, so in the morning when Garren dressed to work in the field, he put on high-top work shoes and purple shorts made specially for him from a pattern used in Guatemala. He must have looked strange and exotic. And comic. A tall bony-faced Irishman, with coarse light hair and a suntan, crinkly lines around his blue eyes and a loin cloth and shoes. He wouldn't have looked like a colonialist because his face was naturally innocent, not an owner's face, a face easily surprised. Nearly a quarter-century after he bought the tractor, he could still be happy to find it there in the barn, his, this wonderful machine.

That morning he had breakfast with Nell. The sun made their land bright and beautiful. They sat comfortably over their cereal and coffee, she with her correspondence spread out before her in the breakfast alcove of their farmhouse, he with the newspaper. Nell was not a bad-looking woman. But in the twenty-odd years they'd had the farm, her body and hair gradually took on the protective coloring of the place. Her hair went to its natural straw color, then some gray came in. Her body became rounder, soft, less defined. She couldn't be bothered with makeup, unless she had to go into a city for one of his openings.

The sun shone brilliantly on them as they sat at breakfast. Almost everybody they knew thought they'd found the perfect life. Garren got up and brought his paperwork to the table, signed a contract for a show of his photographs, paid bills, ordered film, took care of business, thought about Denise. Then he and Nell stirred themselves and like two good comrades went to work outdoors.

Now, here's how the land outside the house was. It's important in picturing the accident. If you looked at a map or took an aerial photograph, in the northwest corner would be a pond. The algae had killed the fish, so there were no more trout or black bass, but there were some friendly water snakes. In the northeast corner was the barn. The second floor was all storage—books, furniture, and old, old photos, packed away for safety. The barn was also, of course, where the tractor was kept. It lived amidst the chain saw, tools, other farm equipment, and things to service the tractor. In the middle plane of this map of ours was the house, at the west, then the yard, then a stream cutting a diagonal from the pond northwest of the house to the rented fields in the south. Right in the center, next to the stream, was the grass that Garren went to cut. That grass was next to the stream Nell was going to work in. To the east of all that was a lovely vegetable garden, which Garren had put in. Well, it must have been lovely.

"Damn, look at this mess," Garren said, looking toward the rented-out land to the south. The farmer who rented the fields used so much fertilizer that there was a nitrogen build-up which, although it was great for the corn in Garren's garden, made the weeds and algae in the stream go absolutely crazy. The weeds were Nellie's job. She wore Garren's thigh-high rubber wading boots for tromping in the stream. She was to pull up those weeds. As he went for the tractor, Garren saw how she wobbled along, lifting each boot with each step. All morning, Garren worked beside her, in a manner of speaking, on the tractor, cutting the high grass. The morning represented their marriage.

The accident happened after lunch. Afternoon: This was his life with Denise. They had come back and worked an hour or two more; so it was mid-afternoon and they were probably tired. Garren was a hard worker.

The sickle bar on the tractor started the whole accident. It was five feet long, made up of metal shark teeth. It was held by a chain, but a lever pulled the chain so you could lift the bar when going over a rock. Mid-afternoon, when Garren had occasion to pull the lever, a link of the chain broke, and the sickle bar fell to the ground. This bar was heavy, eighty pounds or so. Garren got off the tractor, turned off the sickle bar by first shutting the engine off. He had no brake system on this old machine. He'd become more or less used to that. So he put the tractor in gear so it would hold on the hill. He got off, walked to the barn, and fetched wire to tie up the bar. He planned to drive the tractor back to the barn where he would use an acetylene torch to weld the chain back together. Garren had become handy at things around the farm, although it appeared less and less his kind of life. He got the bar tied up. Then, he did something stupid. Instead of getting on the tractor to start the engine, he started it from the ground while standing in front of the rear left wheel. Now he'd done this thousands of times with the tractor in neutral. However, he'd forgotten somehow that he had the thing in first gear. He was tired, despairing, looking for a way out of his marriage. Images of Denise came to him, mirages in the heat. She was water. He pushed the clutch pedal with his hand, reached up over the little hood to the starter button. The thing was in first gear so it started forward.

Garren was wearing heavy work boots and, otherwise, just that little diaper. He started backing up as fast as possible. There was nothing to hold onto. Nellie didn't see. Nellie continued to pull weeds. He couldn't call out. He kept backing up, running backward and the tractor kept moving and yet for a while, maybe only a few seconds, he kept escaping. Then he tripped. The tractor, inexorable, being a tractor, kept coming on, kept at him.

Garren understood that the wheel would go over him. He tried to pull himself into a fetal position. Even though he was adjusting his body in a desperate attempt to live, he saw the big wheel come over him and thought, "This is it. Well, at least it won't take long. I'll go quickly."

Nellie said later she heard a scream and turned from her weeding.

Garren doesn't remember screaming at all. The wheel went up over his outer thighs, over his hip, over his upper arm, over his inner shoulder. He inflated his body, like a tire, pumping up with breath, to fend off the attack. He blacked out. He swam in blackness. For a long time. Forever.

Then he was sitting up, and a part of him understood what had happened. He became his own medic—reached out to feel his legs, arms, ribs for broken bones, wondered about internal bleeding.

Probably only a split second had gone by.

Nellie had heard the scream and she was trying to run toward him, but she was wearing his old rubber boots and she couldn't move very fast. She was like a Marx brother in slow motion.

Meanwhile, Garren was sitting up, somehow realizing that the determined tractor, which had pivoted over his shoulder and miraculously missed his head, now headed toward the tender evergreens he'd planted. He felt no pain. He yelled to Nellie, "For God's sake, stop the tractor." He imagined it going, eating everything in its way, all the way to Poughkeepsie.

Nellie waddled off after it, trying to stop it while it was going. The ground was uneven, and it was dangerous for her to get so close to the tractor which, mindless, might pivot again at any time, but somehow she got to it and stalled it. Maybe she pulled the throttle back. Then Nell made her way, in the big boots, back to Garren. He said, "Call the volunteer ambulance." He wanted to move, but he knew he shouldn't, so he sat there. His son's dog, Casey—named for Stengel, and gotten as a puppy, part golden retriever, part Chesapeake, now very large—came up and took the spoon position inside him to keep him warm. He petted Casey and thought he was going to cry, the dog's love was so pure.

Nell called the fire company that operated a volunteer ambulance. They were farmers, mill workers, ordinary citizens, good folks. The word went out on the radio that there was an emergency at Garren's farm. He was a popular guy in the district, a character with his loin cloths and his funny family name—not Gary, not Garrett, not Darren. And who knows, maybe nothing else was happening that day. Anyway four ambulances from four towns came screaming and screeching up the road to the fields. Casey snarled at all of them; the ambulance men couldn't get near Garren. Finally Nell coaxed the dog away. The local men got the honors, pulled out a big board and strapped Garren to it. They took him to a hospital in the city of Hudson, thirty-five miles away.

The tractor, they all estimated on the way to the hospital, was a ton and a half, two tons.

In the emergency room, women oohed and aahed about the purple Guatemalan fisherman's breeches. Garren explained from his prone position that he had seen a pattern in a magazine, liked it, and taken it to a local woman who sewed for a living. He had two made, he told them, purple and white.

The women said, "Imagine that!" And "We'll have to have you model your white ones too, sweetie. But honey, these are coming off."

They began to move him. He felt as if he were in a coffin but awake. They put him into a scanner. He could hear doctors gathering. He could make out, "spleen, broken bones, vital organs." The pictures they wanted to get took several hours. Garren thought it was probably too late, that after all this they'd find something unfixable, and he'd die anyway.

The doctors murmured.

At the end of it, they told him it was a miracle. They couldn't understand how he was still alive, but they could find nothing wrong. They theorized soberly that the heavy grass had apparently acted like a cushion. They told him, "You are one very lucky man. We're going to release you. You go home and go to bed. We don't want you to do *anything* for days." They gave him a pile of pain killers. Looked envious.

Nellie took him home. She mixed him a martini and made him a wonderful dinner of fresh vegetables from the garden and a small veal roast. The house smelled terrific from the food. The whole county phoned to see how he was. He felt immortal.

But best of all was Nell who moved in and out of the room, checking on him. He was so grateful to be alive. "Nell," he said. "Nellie." It's as if he'd wanted this moment with her all along, for a long time. He looked at her and he felt happy. Their whole life together, their marriage, made sense. Their children had issued from their bodies. Their son's dog, Casey, loved them all, would have leaped to protect any one of them. Their hairs were turning gray together. Yes, this was his life and it was good.

Still, when he thought about what almost happened, his death, one awful thing was imagining that for a long time, probably for a very long time, Denise would not have any idea why she no longer heard from him. Nobody would have known to call her. She would have thought he stopped caring about her. She would have sat on her own bed, one knee up, reading photography journals, one after another, pressing herself to blot out the rejection. Weeks would go by. She wouldn't eat very much. She would do nothing but study. Somebody would come by with drugs. She'd say, great. Even while he was confined to bed, he thought, she might suffer some damage not hearing from him. As evening moved into night, he found other thoughts intruding on his happiness over being alive. He remembered Nell's critical tone. He heard her brother, a hardened cynic who played at folksiness, say, "You still tinkering with that camera?" and "Hey, haven't you heard, they've got color film now!" He thought about how neither Nellie nor her family had a clue who he was or what he was trying to do.

What would Denise think, today, tomorrow, when there were no phone calls? He lay in bed remembering her lovely pixie face, tiny strong body, her sadness, mostly her sadness, for no matter how carelessly she dropped expensive clothing on chairs and tilted her head with that quizzical coolness, she was sad. Almost all the time. It was an odd and mighty aphrodisiac.

He would manage to get up and out of the house and he would call her.

Terrible guilt took the form of Nell entering their room with a flower in a vase and a piece of pie. Garren watched her through the haze of pain killers, again thrilled and touched that she loved him.

II

Garren and I are on a plane high in the clouds on our way to San Francisco where we will attend a photographer's conference. (I'm a photographer, too. That's how I met Garren.) Years have passed since the tractor accident, nearly ten in fact. Garren has changed his life, left the farm, divorced Nell, and made a very impressive career as a photographer. Then after a couple of emotionally turbulent years, he stopped trying to fly out to San Francisco to see Denise. He tried other relationships for a while. And then I came along.

We've been together for three years and we're headed toward marriage. Things have been pretty good. I haven't had many doubts. But whenever the tractor accident comes up, I feel the ground shift. I get scared. I lose my love for Garren. I want to run away. So why do I keep prodding him about it? Why did I ask him about it today? Well, for one thing, Denise may very well be at this conference. Some of her photographs are on exhibit, and she now lives in San Francisco. She lingers in Garren's life like a late afternoon light in autumn. A letter here, a card there.

And I guess I think that somewhere in the story is the right glimpse of him, one I can hold onto when I get doubts, something that will make my fears go away.

The one thing I can't get him to say is that Denise didn't actually love him or at least that she didn't love him enough. He's told me about the tractor accident maybe three or four times before today, but today I pore over the facts all over again.

And not just the facts. Images, too. We are halfway through the trip, halfway across the country, between the two coasts. We are surrounded by clouds. I think of Nell as belonging to the East Coast (and not just geographically), Denise to the West Coast. My personality is somewhere around Chicago. My age splits the difference between these other two women as well. We are in my territory.

For some reason the clouds that surround us make me think of the field hay.

I stand and make my way through the swaying plane to the bathroom, imagining that I am magically suspended, walking through clouds, then driving through field hay. I tractor my way through. The mirror in the lavatory reminds me that I am solid and sensible. Then I tractor my way back to Garren. He has chosen to wear a clay-red and putty colored sweater I bought him. It's cotton, smooth, of an intricate design. Under it is an ivory shirt. Khakis. He turns a few heads, but I don't think he's ever quite realized it. When I get back to my seat, he is looking with interest at the flight magazine. As I slip in, he looks up, happy.

We and all the other passengers have been lulled by the airlines into losing track of time. First magazines, newspapers, coffee. Then breakfast. Then stereo headphones and a movie. *Ransom* is the feature of the day. Garren and I aren't watching. We're watching the tractor accident instead.

"How will you feel when you see her? If you see her," I ask. I know Denise gets under the skin, leaves people unsettled.

Garren takes my hand. "Julia, I love you now," he says. He smiles sweetly, but in the afterimage of the smile, for just a split second, the Denise part of him smells blood.

I don't know why I had to start asking about that part of Garren's life. Even as I asked, I felt it was self-destructive, because Garren tells this incident in a detached way and the detachment upsets me. If he would show some feeling, some regret, I would be all right. But when I see this distant side of him, when I hear him recount the facts of his betrayal of his wife, I forget that he has changed my life for the better, that he is kind, and often really funny, and certainly bright and interesting. The part of his life before the divorce, the years of alienation, terrify me. I suppose, 'Could this happen again?' is the question that haunts me. Because Denise, I figure, is a part of him. Just as I am, just as Nell is. And what Denise represents, to my mind, is his selfishness, a death-defying selfishness. What's even more awful is that I understand it.

And so we have had an accident, too. I've caused it. I've brought all this up. And now Denise has fallen across our path like the five-foot-long, shark-toothed sickle bar, something we must fix correctly or it will cause a bigger accident.

"We were at the part where you were at home in bed trying to figure out how to call Denise," I prompt. I'm watching myself. Couldn't I have asked that differently? I wonder if the people behind the high-backed seats have heard me.

But Garren has little sense of our publicness. "Well," he says, rewinding the tape, "I felt immortal. Nellie sat on the edge of the bed and we held hands. I never loved her so much as I did then. We talked about all kinds of things. Then I fell asleep on martinis and painkillers. It was a really deep sleep. But about four in the morning I woke up with the most awful stomach pain. I thought, 'This is it. It's something they haven't found. I'm going to die from it after all.'"

"Did you really believe that?"

"I don't know. Maybe. Yes, I did."

"Okay."

"You still want me to tell this?" he asks.

"Yes. Everything."

"*Nothing* was working. None of my systems. Everything was traumatized, rigid. Anyway Nell called the volunteers again and they took me back to the hospital. They gave me more tests and threw up their hands. They couldn't find anything wrong, but they granted I was in terrible pain. They concluded I had gas. Pretty embarrassing. So they gave me Demerol and I went into happy land. I mean, really happy. Then I'd awake in agony. They'd give me more Demerol. Happy, very happy. Then agony. More Demerol. It went on like that."

I've seen Garren wave aside ordinary aches and pains: cuts, bruises, burns. He hardly notices he has them. So he really was hurting. But this is not it, not the aperture through which I find my good feelings again. I see his kidneys, his stomach, his pancreas, his intestines, like so many cartoon characters, mowed down, flattened, traumatized, unable to plump up again to the right shapes. In cartoons this comes about magically in a frame.

"The nurse would come in and say, 'Roll over, sweetheart.' She'd jab me, and I'd have sweet dreams again."

"When you came to, did you think about Denise?"

"Well, I must have. I wrote a letter from the hospital and somehow got it mailed. I remember that. I couldn't make a phone call. A doctor came in and said, 'We don't know what it is, but something's wrong in there. We'll have to open you up.' So I wasn't moving around much. Although I do remember walking around with an IV on a wheeler. Grittily cheerful, just unable to perform the necessary functions."

"And still in pain?"

"Oh, yes. One morning they came and took me to the x-ray room. A couple of the x-ray techs who worked there were Dutchess County farm girls. They were earthy and big. They picked me up and moved me this way and that. And suddenly I left a big fart. The biggest, longest you can imagine. They sent up a big cheer. Word went out into the hallways." He makes an utterly disarming funny face and I laugh, but humor is not the way in either.

"They said, 'Do it again, sweetheart!' They cheered me on. 'Come on, do it again.' I did my best but I never could measure up to that first time."

Surely the people in the seat in front of us are tuned in to us by now or totally out on Demerol.

"Friends came to visit all summer. Eventually I got back to work on the farm. But I never drove the tractor again. It stayed in the field where Nell had stalled it for weeks. Then one day Michael said, 'Let's move it to the barn.' The battery had died. We had to jump start it. I let Michael take it to the barn and park it. I thought, 'No more.'"

This part about not driving the tractor again gets to me. I understand: There was fear, and depression long afterwards.

"By the time I got to Miami, Denise had moved out to San Francisco and things were okay."

"Okay? How do you mean?"

"I felt better. I flew out just about every weekend."

No, no.

"But you said you never trusted her. She sounds like a woman in a gangster movie, beautiful and bad and lying all the time."

"She was. She was just like that. It didn't matter. I knew there was an age difference, a career difference. I was an old guy, she was a young girl. I knew all that. It didn't matter."

"How could it not matter?" I am moving ahead very fast, too fast. "Wait a minute! How can I be sure you've been fair to her? Maybe she's perfectly innocent of half the things you say about her. Maybe she wasn't playing games with you. Maybe she never lied to you."

"No. She did lie. And then she'd admit it later."

"Well, tell me something good about her then. Otherwise, what should I think of you?"

"I owe her a lot," he's saying, overlapping me. "She freed me. She made me see things differently. She was an instrument of change. And I was, too, for her. We had a mutual projection association. I gave her dreams, an image of herself. An idea of achievement. She gave me the idea that I could be who I wanted to be. With her, I didn't feel like a fool. I felt that I had talent and the right to pursue it. I guess she gave me dreams, too. And an idea of achievement. She meant a lot to me. I guess lies were part of it."

"Are you still in danger?" I ask quietly. "I mean you've already told me we could be having a drink in the hotel lobby or going up an elevator and pow, we could run into her." What I really want to ask is, "Am I in danger?"

"No," he says, taking my hand again and kissing it. "I'm not in danger. We're okay."

I want to tie the sickle bar up in place. I want to wind the wire carefully. A stewardess comes by with another snack, a turkey sandwich on a tiny bun. The food distracts us. We eat, drift into naps. And when we wake, Garren takes up where I've been all along, at the questionable character of Denise and that part of his character that she appealed to.

"You see, Denise compartmentalized her life. There were different parts of her and different groups of people in her life. They were separate from each other. I think that's what got her into trouble. She became whoever she was with. I belonged to only one part. She has a lot of personalities. One of them....Well, let's just say she came close to giving me the kind of affection you give me. Even though when I wasn't there, she was filling in with another group of people. Maybe screwing half of them."

"Do you really think so?"

"Oh, yes."

"But you put up with it."

"I think it made me feel safe. Change is such a hard thing."

The stewardesses take our little trays, our headphones.

"If you meet her, you'll like her," he says.

"What will I see in her that I'll like?"

"Oh...a little part of yourself, I expect. A woman who's been hurt and used again and again, trying to turn the tables."

But I haven't had it so bad, I think. A marriage with a guy who ran around on me and lied about it. And yes, I'm scared. But I never got so bad I had to knock myself out on chemicals.

"You see a similarity?" I ask.

"Yes," he challenges, "there's something that's similar."

What can I say? I sense it's true. It has something to do with this driving the tractor through the clouds of field hay, not looking left or right, just cutting. Why? To get rid of whatever's in the way. To see.

"Denise will probably be a little afraid of you. She's always trying to be special."

"That's dangerous." I manage a smile.

The plane tilts to the right and we begin to descend. We leave the clouds behind, like smoke.

"You'll meet Nell, too, one day. It's inevitable. And you'll like her."

"How do you know?"

"I just do. For one thing, she'll want you to like her. She'll say funny things. She'll want to be tough and witty, a character. Buddy-buddy. That's how she is. That's how she gets through things. She's a really good person, one of the most generous people you could ever meet."

What a strange face he makes. It looks like real regret. I look into Garren's eyes, and I see our West coast experience—Denise braving out a meeting with me. Then what? Nell running in slow motion in the big boots. She looks pretty funny. But nice. And yes, I like her.

MARIA

John Barnes is afraid this driver, this woman, Lynn Stroub, will hit a child or a dog because she turns back to face him much of the time, talking and talking, even when she turns down the steep cobblestone street in San Miguel de Allende. On the two-hour drive from San Luis Potosi (it should have been three), she told him all about her sex life, or maybe it was actually a love life, while creating a third, passing, lane between speeding trucks. Lynn Stroub has a pointed nose and spiky hair, eyes that stay open a fraction of an inch too wide. John Barnes thinks of her as some ancient spirit carrying him to a new place. But he's prone to romantic thoughts. She's actually only an American, like him, getting away from something. She makes a living meeting planes, driving tourists, transporting baggage.

Moments ago she turned from a dirt road to a surprisingly wide tree-lined street, where he saw old cars, trucks, and buses spewing exhaust fumes, and then just as suddenly to this steep and crowded street of cobblestones. They have to wait, idling. Just in front of them, one car squeezes around another. People actually carry things on their heads! At least one woman—a caryatid with a table top of vegetables. Has she been selling them? Before he can see everything he wants to see—the groups of children playing, the stucco houses, the heavy doorways—Lynn Stroub has made her way through and past the people and the cars to the bottom of this hilly street where there is a tree in the middle of the road. Her Colt squeezes around it, and there they are, before a door, a very newly painted, heavy door. His hacienda. For a time. For five months. People have told him there might be anything behind these blank doors and stucco walls—from mini-ghettos to elaborately gardened estates.

"I've never seen inside this one," Lynn Stroub says. Her eyes widen greedily at the prospect. She wants to know what she is missing.

In the next moments, John Barnes meets two more women: Shauna, the expatriate owner of the property, and another woman, whom he knows by the fact that she scurries under their feet, to be María. Shauna has explained María comes with the rental. Barnes is uncomfortable about having a maid at all, but to refuse her is a problem, too. It would deprive her of a job and him of needed time to write his book. Still, it dismays him to watch María lift his cases of notes. They are so heavy that *he* hates to lift them. María works; Shauna Walters holds him with what she, no doubt, believes to be a line of polite social interaction. She drifts around the garden, dangling a set of keys and showing him which trees are new, which bushes will flower, as she asks him about his trip. He quietly admires the silk pants outfit she wears and thinks his ex-wife would have liked it. He wonders why Shauna is so decked out in the middle of a weekday afternoon. He tries to catch María's eyes to indicate that he is friendly and will treat her well, but she escapes him.

A week later, much settled into routine, Barnes looks glumly at the house from the table in the garden. It is just his luck to come to an exotic place and end up with a house that is pure suburban New Jersey. There isn't a bookcase or a reading lamp anywhere, not to mention a book or a magazine. Everything is perfect, predictable, blandly marble as if the owners have reproduced their Formica, plastic, and pressed board in this new place, but with better materials. He sits among flowers, eating fresh tomatoes, a Mexican-made Brie, and crusty bread. As other Americans have hurried to tell him, he can find almost anything here, tucked away in tiny shops. He hears María tiptoe across the marble floors of the kitchen to peer out the screen door. Is it time to remove his plate? her look asks. No, he motions, a hand held up to halt her, he wants to linger over the last few bites.

And besides he is writing a letter. He is writing to his ex-wife, trying to give her the picture of a man who is not boring. He laughs at himself. Callie will probably read the thing in the company of some architect, some actor, some travel agent, who has the ability to fascinate her. He writes this letter, he tells himself, simply to report on the town she'd once wanted to visit. It's charming, he says, hot springs outside the town, clothing boutiques on every street, an incredible maid named María who washes clothes by hand and gets out all the spots no dry cleaner has been able to get out. He would like to tell her about the poverty around him, the difference in lifestyles between the Americans and the Mexicans, and ironically which of the two groups seems the happier, but he knows she is less likely to find him interesting when he writes about such things. So he gives her the tourist goods.

Yet, when he reads over the letter, he filters it through Callie's eyes and realizes she will still find him boring. Boring, boring. The hell with it. She will never love him again. He gets up from the table, carrying his own plates.

"*María?*" he calls.

"*Sí, señor?*" She runs from somewhere, takes the plates from his hands even though he is trying to hold onto them.

"Have something to eat. Sit out here if you'd like. There's chicken, Brie, bread, tomatoes, whatever you'd like."

"*Gracias, señor.*"

María is very small and square. She has a full face and not much of a waist. She might have been carved out of a rectangular block of brown wood. On most days she wears simple polyester pants with a shirt tucked in. These clothes are clean and pressed, not very colorful. Her long black hair is combed straight back and caught in an elastic band. There is something serene in her clean, plain squareness. He likes having María in and about the house. When he goes downstairs from the room he uses as his study, he finds her trimming the indoor plants, mopping the floors, giving the stove an extra wiping. If he reads outdoors, he might go upstairs to change a shirt and find her folding the laundry or ironing. If he needs to *be* upstairs in the late part of the day, he can hear her on the service deck scrubbing the spots out of his clothes at the old washing board. She is always on alert, always busy, always out of the way but still there. Yes, he understands that he is lonely. He wonders what her husband does for a living. He imagines that because she is so orderly and her own clothes are well cared for, almost fashionable, too, that she lives with an energetic man named Juan or Ràul. He sees them sitting up late at night, budgeting, figuring. He determines to leave her a large tip when he goes home.

He has met yet another woman in this first week. Bibi Richter in many ways resembles Callie. It's almost the first thing he thought about her when he met her at a party he was lucky enough to be invited to on his second day in town.

"Everybody has a favorite beggar," she was saying. "I give to the blind woman at the corner of Hernández Macías and Quadrante."

He shivered at her phrasing, and yet, in spite of himself, he found himself drawn to her. Maybe out of old habit. She had a strong confident voice that carried in crowds. One of his colleagues would have described her as a woman who had appropriated white male values in the feminine atmosphere of the third world. But Barnes thought there was more to her than that. He sensed a sweetness under some sort of discomfort. He planned to call Bibi and ask her to dinner or something. But a few days after the party, he is wandering up the hill, being jostled by laborers moving stones. He is smelling restaurant pizza and chicken along the way and looking into shop windows at small boxes of Tide and muslin shirts. At the top, he has just handed a few coins to the blind woman when he turns into another street and sees Bibi on her way to the corner, casually emptying her pockets as she walks. She calls to him and asks him to join her for coffee at The French Place.

Bibi is blonde, cheerful, clothed expensively and with theatrical dash. Today she wears triangular hand-painted earrings in the Mexican combinations used for flower arrangements—red, orange, pink. A scarf dominated by those colors falls carelessly around her shoulders. Bibi, dawdling over the menu, watching others, reading fliers announcing an upcoming lecture, skimming the newspaper, acts as if she's known John Barnes for years. She is cozily domestic. This is like breakfast together between old marrieds. Given her resemblance to Callie, it's odd, funny, intriguing. But how will it help him to exorcise Callie?

It turns out Bibi knows something about María. "She has six children, last I heard. No husband, of course, they never do. Just babies, one after the other. You'd think they'd learn."

Barnes is surprised but can't for the world figure out why he hasn't thought of this to begin with. María works like a woman who has never been cared for. He wants to buy her something. A scarf, a watch. Something pretty.

"She's quite a religious girl, your María. Goes on pilgrimages, one after the other. Ask her what she's doing on her day off and it's likely to be a twenty mile walk at midnight to see some Christ figure on a cross. Amazing stamina."

"I'm impressed with her," he tells Bibi. "She's very alert, very responsible. Imagine how much she has to manage. And she always looks perfect and she's always on time. Six children! To support!"

"Oh, I'm sure they fend for themselves. The girls learn to wash clothes when they're seven or so. The boys are pretty worthless. They're in training to grow up and leave women pregnant, just like their fathers did. But by the time they're five, they stay out of the house most of the time."

The croissants are amazingly good at this breakfast place. And the coffee is excellent. Who would have thought to find them here where girls of seven wash clothes instead of going out to play?

"I come here all the time," Bibi says. "Listen. I've got an idea. Would you like to go to a full moon party? It's really a hot springs party just out of town. I could pick you up. It's next Tuesday. Everybody brings something to eat. I've been to other ones. They're fun."

John has nodded acceptance all through her invitation. He doesn't approve of Bibi's breezy tone, but he can't for a moment imagine not following this through. He's on a journey. He felt it when Lynn Stroub drove him into town.

"Would you like to go to dinner this weekend?" he asks.

"Of course," she says. "Of course I'd love to go. John Barnes, John Barnes. What does that name remind me of?"

"It's a very common name. When people want an alias to check into a hotel or to open a fake account, they're as likely to come up with John Barnes as anything. The FBI comes to visit me once a year or so. It's a weird name to have. People assume you're a criminal. I'm always answering which John Barnes I am."

"And which one are you?" Bibi smiles, but her eyes dart away and back, checking on who has just come into the restaurant.

"I'm the one who's writing a book on the politics of upstate New York," he says.

"No kidding! You know about that?"

"Yes. Or I think I do. Otherwise I'd be a fraud. Like those other John Barneses."

"What's your book about?"

"The machines. The clubs. The organizations. A history of the changing terms for the same scratch-my-back operations. America. You see, we think the machines had to go, that they were a bad thing. And in some ways they were. But not all bad. In terms of grooming candidates, that kind of thing, not all bad. I've got a thousand stories to illustrate that."

"Interesting. Well, you mustn't work too hard. See some of the little towns around here. See things."

At the moment, all he can see is her bright colors and Callie, always Callie, behind her, playing hide and seek with him.

"You're paying too much for this place!" Bibi says, a week later, as soon as she enters the house. "It's pretty good, it really is, but Shauna is overcharging you."

"Do you think so? Don't the houses on this row go for quite a lot?"

"Even so." She moves around, inspecting the kitchen. Barnes has no trouble believing Bibi. He goes out of his way to avoid Shauna and senses there is something of the cheat in her. Her face is sneaky. She parades around in her silks and satins, poses with her very large rump towards him, but she finds it difficult to look him straight in the face. Why can't she look at him? And she's always in a hurry, as if she's late for lunch at the Waldorf.

"Your plants are in perfect condition."

"María is fantastic." He opens the drawer of a cabinet in the dining room and takes out a silk scarf. "What do you think? I bought it for María."

"It's gorgeous, but what will she do with it? I hate to crush you, but she'll probably need to sell it. I mean, that would buy her groceries for a month."

"If she needs to sell it, fine. I just thought she should have something pretty, for once in her life." It's no secret that Bibi is looking at him skeptically. Yes, he romanticizes women. But isn't it true that under every hardworking, make-do woman is a lyrical beauty? "Come," he says. "Show me your hot-tub friends."

"Bibi," somebody calls. "Glad you made it."

Barnes slips into the strong-smelling water. The bright moonlight illuminates slabs of rock decked with plates of vegetables, chicken, dips, jugs of margaritas or bottles of wine. Bibi has brought barbecued chicken for both of them—repayment, she says, for the dinner he treated her to over the weekend. The food all around him makes Barnes suddenly hungry, but it would be impolite to dive straight for it so he joins a group of people who are engaged in a desultory conversation and who look at him as if he is unwelcome. Once among them, he doesn't feel like swimming away, so he stands his ground. Everyone wears swimming clothes except two men in the group Barnes joined. He sees their genitals lazily bobbing with the movement of the water. One of the men, surely drunk, is telling laconically how he left the rat race behind and brought his family to live down here. Barnes wonders what the family lives on. Behind him, Bibi's voice rises shrill with laughter.

There are three connected pools at this hot springs. At one point, Barnes, swimming from one to the other, encounters Lynn Stroub. She and a man he doesn't know are eating something rapidly, desperately. "*Tamales*," she says apologetically. "Bill had his maid make them. We only have these two. Would you like a little taste?"

Barnes manages to refuse. He wants a whole tamale! And is afraid he will gobble as desperately as they do if they give him a little taste. For a moment he thinks he sees his landlady, Shauna. Then he realizes she would find this party beneath her. He finds it beneath him too, but hopefully for different reasons.

Bibi slips an arm around him and kisses him. Desire flares up and he knows he will follow it, can't help but follow it, he is so lonely and it's so familiar, her gesture, so like Callie, that it's almost as if Bibi isn't a stranger at all.

"It'll be a nice thing, this," Bibi says late in the night in her bed as they shelter against the night breeze. Her hair is still damp, and it is matted, as his is, and they both still smell of sulfur. She is lovely, has a trim body and an eager look on her face. "Five months," she adds. "It'll be good for both of us."

Barnes doesn't tell her that he falls in love easily or that he is almost too hurt already by the matter-of-fact temporariness of this affair to go on with it. He stares thoughtfully at the ceiling. Perhaps this is all part of whatever he has to work through, put behind him.

"How's the book?"

"Slow. I wanted to work eight hours a day, but I wear out after six. Still, if I keep at it, I should have a draft by the time I leave. I'll have a little time once I get back to do some revisions before the term starts."

"Are you up for tenure?"

"Oh, no, I have that."

"Will you have to look for a publisher?"

"I've got one." He laughs. "Nothing much wrong with my life, huh?"

"You're quite a success." Bibi shivers and snuggles down.

Does she think so? He doesn't want to give any false impressions. So he says, "I'm getting over a failed marriage. I only tell you because it might hit me in the face sometime when I least expect it. I want to get past it and all that. It's just that I still get depressed."

Uncanny. Bibi strokes his thigh just as Callie would have done, a comforting move that disconcerts him.

The only person with whom he does not feel boring is María. He gives her the scarf and she blushes and dips several times in bows of thanks. The blush is especially apparent in her eyes. She looks at the scarf, lifts it carefully, feels it with the back of her hand because, she indicates, her fingertips are callused and scratchy and she is afraid to touch it. He has not seen anyone clean as hard as she cleans since he was a boy and his grandmother did everything—floors, windows, the pipes beneath the sinks—with cloths dipped in chemical solutions. He takes the scarf and puts it around her neck. She flushes again. He takes it up and shows her how it would look on her ponytail. He can feel the dampness of her hair where it's caught by the rubber band.

She shakes her head as if to say, "Such a beautiful thing on my hair? Never!" She wears a pair of creased brown pants and a short-sleeved red knit top, which contrast with the colors in the scarf—Callie's complex purples, pinks, and blues, brilliant and shimmering with light.

Where does she buy her sturdy clothes? How does she keep them so neat? He hopes she will wear the scarf. But if she does, he never sees her in it. She continues to dress in the same way for work, to dip and bow her head as she passes him. Each morning, he tries to catch her with a friendly hello before she bows. He looks back quickly to his work so she will not greet him as a servant.

One day she stands behind him and watches him work. At this point he is still writing his manuscript by hand. *"Hay muchos papeles, muchas hojas,"* she says admiringly. Then when he begins to revise and type, putting the thing onto a computer disk, she stops every once in a while to watch the computer work. *"Dónde están las hojas?"* she asks, fingers to her mouth.

In an elaborate pantomime, he tells her they are now in the machine, *"la computadora,"* which *"no olvida."*

She looks at him skeptically and laughs, which makes him laugh.

He tries to tell all this to Bibi whose off-hand response is, again, just like Callie. "Oh, she hasn't seen one of those before. But she's smart, so I've heard. Don't think she'll forget it."

"How do you know she's smart?"

"These people I know, Mel and Linesse—they're artsy types, so I don't know whether we'll run into them at parties or not, probably not—but they're on a committee with me and I remember she used to work for them. Probably still does."

"María? She works for me six days a week."

"Maybe she squeezes in two or three more jobs, you never know."

María comes to Barnes ten to four o'clock some days and twelve to six o'clock on others.

"Mornings. I think she worked for them in the early mornings."

He manages to ask María if she has *"otro trabajo."* After a while she understands that he means, *"otro empleo."* When she admits that she does, she looks frightened, and he understands that she is worried he finds her work unsatisfactory. *"No, no,"* he hastens to tell her in a mixture of pantomime, English, and Spanish. "You must get very tired, *cansada.* Six kids and all. *Seis niños."*

She shakes her head.

Later that day she asks him if everything is all right.

He tells her yes, everything is wonderful. He feels happy because Callie has answered his letter and because she has wished him well. And tonight her incarnation is waiting to serve him dinner and to take him to a lecture.

When he sees María look at her left wrist, which is bare, and then go to the kitchen to look at the clock, he assumes that he has frightened her about keeping to exact hours. "No, no," he says, ushering her out. "Go." He tumbles over himself trying to tell her not to worry about time and also asking her why she has no wristwatch. *"Ha olvidado su reloj?"*

She explains in slow Spanish that her watch, a gift from her employer Shauna, has been lost. Lost. *"Lo he perdido. Perdido."* Her face shows distress. Somewhere on the street, she pantomimes. Her right hand shows the watch lifting off from her wrist and falling to the pavement.

"Terrible," he says, shaking his head. *"Qué color?"*

"Negro," she says.

He cannot find her a black watch, so on the way to Bibi's house, he buys her a white one and slips it into his pocket. Perhaps by the time he leaves town, he will have found a black one somewhere. Then she'll have two.

"She probably sold it," Bibi tells him, not without a little pique. "But of course she can't admit it, she has to say she lost it. And she's probably afraid of Shauna. The whole town is, actually."

He, too, is a little afraid of Shauna, without knowing why. "What would Shauna do to her?"

"Lord knows. She's a screamer. You should hear her at the school board, at the delicatessen, in shops. What a temper.

She's always right, everyone else is wrong. She'd make your María miserable somehow, you'd better believe it." They don't actually go into Bibi's house to eat dinner but settle at the table in the courtyard, surrounded by flowers.

"You seem to know everything about everybody," John Barnes says, sitting down. "I've never even seen Shauna's husband."

"Well, I've been here for twenty years, off and on. I do know just about everything. Her husband's a handsome guy. I remember seeing him around before she ever met him. Before my divorce, my husband and I used to come here on vacation. Then after the settlement, I couldn't afford much of a lifestyle in the States, so I came back. Everybody comes back. That's what they say."

He has wondered about her, wondered when she would tell him more than the simple fact of her divorce.

"You live very well," he said.

"I wouldn't if I were in the States." She is between forty and fifty years old, as he is, and young-looking as well. Yet she refers to herself as retired. He can't imagine retiring. For Bibi, everything is stopped, settled. This a disturbing thing about her.

For the first time he asks Bibi if she has children and he expects the answer to be no because that's what Callie would answer.

But Bibi surprises him, with a "Goodness, yes. Two boys. They're grown and out of college. Thank God! They're earning livings now, and I don't have to support them." She starts into the house, motioning for him to be still.

"Didn't you ever think of working?" he asks a little loudly, calling after her.

"*Living* is work. Here. I've got a carrot salad, tomatoes, a beans and rice dish and a little chicken." She brings out two plates, already prepared.

"You shouldn't have gone to the trouble," he says.

"Oh, I didn't. I had my girl do it today. She does something with the chicken that makes it very tender." Bibi cocks her head, plunks down the plates, sighs, heads back inside before Barnes can find a way to tell her the way she talks about Mexicans grates on his skin. He wonders, during her brief absence, if he wants to go on seeing her.

She emerges again, brings a bottle of wine to the table. "Actually," she says, "I wangled myself a job with Bird's Eye for a while, but it was pretty unpleasant. I replaced a Mexican foreman and the workers there never forgave me. I finally quit."

Again it happens. Callie's manifestation. Something about Bibi's face—it is closed—keeps him from asking more. Callie, too, had had trouble at work, bitterness and difficulty making a place for herself.

He and Bibi talk about her marvelous garden and the tastiness of the meal. They come around, once more, to María, who, he explains, does the most gorgeous flower arrangements but has never cooked for him. For some reason her contract does not include cooking. "I wonder how old María is?" he asks. "Forty, I'd guess."

"Probably more like thirty-two. Her oldest son is about sixteen, so that makes it about thirty-two."

"A formulaic life," he comments.

"Yes," she laughs. "Predictable, at least. Listen. You're not thinking of dumping me for her, are you?"

"No. I'm just trying to understand her. I wonder about her circumstances. How many fathers do you think there were for the six kids?"

"Probably six."

"Really?"

"Don't be shocked. The guys just don't stick around. It's just how it is."

Is María sad, he wonders. Angry? Did she fall in love easily, get hurt easily? And how does she manage to raise six children on whatever she makes by cleaning? He assumes it is about a hundred dollars a week.

"Maybe some of the fathers provide support," he suggests.

Bibi shakes her head. She stands up and kisses him on the forehead, leaning over to do it. He feels foolish. She is leaning over him, rubbing lipstick off his forehead. All he can see is her hand, which holds her brightly printed blazer away from the table so that it will not bump into any of the food.

"Sweet, foolish John Barnes."

"How much do you think Shauna pays her a week?"

"Oh, I think it's by the month. I think it'd be something like twenty-eight or thirty a month. I pay my girl thirty-five because she's been with me a long time."

"Ah! That's not enough! It's not enough."

Bibi nods. "But to them it's a lot."

All the way to the lecture, John reviews the prices of vegetables and eggs he's seen on the streets. No matter how he figures it, he can't get a week's order to come to less than four dollars. And that's just for a few basics. What about other things? Other food? Coffee? Clothes. Rent. María must have special merchants somewhere who cut her a break. He must make sure she eats more at his place. Maybe if he buys extra pastries and breads, she will take some home.

The lecture they go to is about the genius of the Mayan civilization. The lecturer says that he believes the expression *caca* and the word *cocoa* come from the same root.

"But these are English words," Bibi challenges the speaker in the question and answer session. One thing Barnes likes about her is her fearlessness. "How do you explain that?" she asks loudly.

"These two words are amazingly similar the world over."

John Barnes laughs quietly. "Caca is universal," he whispers to Bibi. "I always knew it."

"Cocoa too," she says. "That's a nice thought. At least to a chocoholic like me."

Callie was a chocoholic, so he knows what to do. "We'll have to go for a nice treat after this is through," he says. "Something chocolate."

"I can't say no."

Is it coincidence that the very persons Bibi said he would probably never meet at the parties she takes him to are at the coffee and pastry shop across the street from the Bellas Artes? Bibi says, "Oh, there are the folks María used to work for. Let's go in there and let me introduce you."

They are Mel Wechsler and Linesse Solomon, a married couple. Mel has a small goatee and wispy thin hair. He is slight but muscular. Linesse is a wide-hipped earthy woman with flowing hair. She wears a long cotton skirt and an almost-nothing cotton tee shirt, which shows she wears no bra and does not shave under her arms.

"We have something in common," he tells them. "I think my maid was your maid. María."

"Gómez? Oh, you must be the man she talks about?" Mel says, settling into a seat at the table.

"So our María is your María!" Linesse says.

"She talks about me?" John looks from one to the other. Mel answers. "She says you work very hard. She tells us about your big manuscript and your computer."

"It's the first she's seen a computer work."

"Oh, no, we have one. We've had one for years. She's seen ours."

"Well, she seemed to be fascinated by mine."

"She's fascinated in general."

"Oh. I see. She just humors me, huh?" He winces as a waiter begins to approach them. "Chocolate, of course, for you," he tells Bibi.

"You'd better believe it."

"Or caca," Linesse says. "I think that guy was full of it. I think he's working the Americans for money for his next dig."

"Oh, you were over there, too. Listen, let me treat," Barnes offers because the Wechsler-Solomons look to be in reduced circumstances. And besides he likes them and hopes to get to know them.

"Thank you," Mel says, studying the menu. "We'll buy next time. We're bound to see you around town."

By the end of the evening, John Barnes knows María works for the Wechsler-Solomons and their family every morning for four hours before coming to work for him. He can't figure out the size of the Wechsler-Solomon family, however, since sometimes they refer to two children, sometimes to sixteen. It takes him two months to sort it out fully. Bibi knows part of the story (that they are always surrounded by a brood), but the Wechsler-Solomons begin to tell him more as he runs into them at the cafe or at breakfast. It turns out they have two children of their own. But they also count a family of eight that has been orphaned when their mother, who lived next door, was run over by a car. The Wechsler-Solomons support these children, feed them, give them clothes, pay for their schooling. And then there are others. Intelligent children from the neighborhood who weren't getting much of a break until the Wechsler-Solomons came along and paid for their education. At first, John thinks this couple must be rich, the version of rich that dresses down. But Mel and Linesse are open about everything.

"We have combined incomes from trusts of $20,000 a year. On that we travel back and forth to the States a few times a year and we buy whatever we need for us and the children. It's plenty, really. We don't need fancy clothes. Clothes are silly."

Indeed they never wear anything but the few pieces he first saw them in. It turns out that four of the children they support are María's four youngest.

"The two oldest boys are worthless," Linesse says. "They're going to be just like their fathers."

The generosity of Mel and Linesse appeals to Barnes enormously. He finds his heart opening around them. María's hard work and courage appeal to him too. He catches himself thinking about her. Wondering what she has to eat on Sundays.

One Sunday he sees her walking home from church with a little girl. The child wears a crisp light blue flowered dress with a lace collar. María wears a straight black skirt and a lacy blue blouse. He runs to catch up with her, to meet her youngest daughter, a beautiful child who smiles shyly and moves closer to her mother. "Lovely," he says. He wishes he could know them better. Why is that so difficult?

Later he finds out through Mel and Linesse that little Linda is María's favorite. "Oh, yes, there's quite a story there!" Mel and Linesse tell him over breakfast one brilliantly sunny morning at a restaurant a few notches down from The

French Place. Their table is set up on the sidewalk. They can look down the hill to the stirring of people, traffic, exhaust fumes, or up the hill to a powdery brown mountainside with a cathedral at the top.

Linesse explains, "Linda's father was a seventy-eight year old man with whom María had a relationship for a couple of years. Apparently a nice old guy. The man left María his house when he died."

"She has her own house?" John asks.

"By American standards it's hardly more than a shack, a basic cottage. But María is the envy of all the women she knows. Having a house of her own. The old guy was ecstatic to have a child, his only child all his life, and he was devoted to María. But when he died, she was very matter-of-fact. "He's dead," she told us. "And then she just put in a day of work."

"Oh."

"She's sworn off men," Linesse says. "She says they're not worth the bother. Now that she has a house and six kids she says she doesn't know what she needs a man for. She's quite a character. Our María."

"María?" John asks them. "I haven't seen that side of her." He tries to imagine her making speeches about her liberation from men. "Maybe she'll meet somebody good. Who knows?"

"I wouldn't bet on it," Mel says. "Although it would be nice of course."

"Look at it this way," Linesse says. "We all keep meeting the same people, playing the same scene, over and over again anyway. There were a couple of guys in there who beat up on María. I'm sure she doesn't want to meet up with *them* again." Linesse slides an elastic band from her thick hair and pulls her hair tighter before fastening it again.

"What do you mean about meeting the same people?" John asks her.

"I don't mean reincarnation or anything like that," Linesse says. "Only that we each have probably about ten people who matter to us—maybe not as many in some cases where there have been small families—and we keep finding them over and over again. Quite frankly, Mel here is my brother. The same type. All right, very incestuous and all that." She laughs and shrugs. "And María is my sister. And our kids are my parents. If you think about it, you'll figure it out."

When he first thinks about it, he can't find the resemblances, except that Bibi reminds him of Callie. But one day, sitting in the sun, he finds he can squint his eyes and picture one person through, almost behind, another. The faces and bodies and voices start to blend. Callie and Bibi are versions of his mother's sister who lived with them for a while. Shauna is his mother. It hurts to think this, but it's true. Mel and Linesse are cousins, the twins who always seemed so interesting, so emotionally advanced even when they were only five. And María would be his grandmother, his mother's mother, who had actually raised him for most of the years of his youth. He could remember his grandmother kneeling on the floor to clean, up on a ladder washing windows, a little too heavy to do either comfortably, but always busy, always active, a woman whose love he never doubted. All of his feelings of comfort go back to her. And his aunt, he remembers in this reverie, was glamorous, 1940s glamorous. She allowed him the role of her knight. And he fell effortlessly into it. While his mother was a social climber given to lies and stratagems, his aunt was secretly tender, sometimes whimsical. Yes, that was his world. His father had given up on his mother and left, although he had done his best over the years not to leave John as well. Long, long ago, John knew he couldn't please his mother. He has lately realized that nobody could.

This realization gets him through some of his interactions with Shauna that otherwise might have given him apoplexy. Shauna finds ways of charging him for things that aren't part of the contract: heating oil, the basic phone service, a chipped toilet seat that he knows he didn't chip, a crack in a glass pitcher. And how has she found these things, anyway? She must have come to look at the house when he stayed overnight at Bibi's. It gives him the creeps. He took this place on the understanding that since he arrived on January tenth and was scheduled to leave on June tenth that he owed her five months rent altogether. She told him in mid-April that he would have to pay rent for all of June. "But that's not what we agreed to by phone," he countered.

Then she flashed her silks at him and turned on her heel saying, "It is. By no means are you going to get away with this." And she rushed out the kitchen door, her shoulders at an angle as if he'd hit her.

When he remembers his mother, he understands there is no pleasant way to resolve things with her. It's sad.

But he is all right. Because all of the love that John felt for his grandmother returns to him as he sits in his garden and plays the little game with vision that Linesse and Mel suggested to him. When he feels his grandmother's love, he can dismiss Shauna. He finds this interesting.

María comes to the garden to say good-bye for the weekend. A little shock goes through him. He feels, in addition to everything else, a strong sexual current. He wishes he could bury himself in her squareness, that he could make her soft. He would never act upon such a thing. Still, he recognizes he's come to love her. His María.

On Easter weekend, there is a long parade through the streets that the Americans tell John he should see. It's more a religious procession than a parade. It lasts for hours and hours. Groups of women carry heavy platforms on which are papier-mâché scenes of the Easter story. The children carry a stage with the baby Christ, adult women carry a huge display of Christ's journey with the cross, older women and teenagers do everything in between. There are nearly a hundred displays; the whole town gets involved.

When Barnes takes his place on the crowded street, he sees that each group of women formally and uniformly. Whole groups wear pink, or blue, or black. Women from the ages of twelve or fourteen and upwards wear heels. Every group, no matter what the age, has to struggle to hold up its platform because the displays are massive and made of wood. Women relieve each other.

Barnes finds himself looking for María. And finally, after he has watched the slow, excruciating procession go on for three hours, he sees her, walking with a group, waiting to take her turn at holding up a stage which shows the women at the tomb. She is dressed in white, as everyone in her group is, except for black high heels. She passes him without seeing him. After a moment's hesitation, he pushes through the crowd on the sidewalk keeping time with the part of the parade that includes María. He feels foolish, but when he sees her bid good-bye to the other women and begin to walk very fast through an archway, then an alley, he follows. He wants to know what kind of house she lives in.

She does not turn, she does not see him. He thinks it would have been a good idea to have an Easter basket, a ham, something to offer. But he doesn't want to lose track of her. Finally she reaches a crooked doorway in a small row of houses. Three small children stand at the door. She shooshes them inside and follows. Just as he had imagined—the small nest-like crowdedness of the place, the smell of beans, the warmth generated by seven bodies in a tiny space.

The next week he tells María that he has not had such an Easter in his whole life. He points to his heart to show that thinking about the procession evokes feeling.

"Ah," she says. "*Bueno.*"

In his fifth month in Mexico, he wants to do something for María that will make her happy. Sometimes as he sits at his computer and taps away at his book, which is now coming along really well, he tries to figure out the right way to give her something. She is proud. When he gave her the watch, months before, her face fell and she said, "No!" before she recovered and thanked him.

Shauna will be very angry if he spoils María, as will half the other Americans, since they have to go on employing Mexicans at the usual rate. He talks this over with Bibi and she tells him that, of course, he has to do what his heart prompts him to do, but she advises a tip of fifty dollars, which is enormous in María's terms and amounts to two months pay.

He thinks about Bibi a good deal as well. They spend several days a week together and are thought of around town as a couple. And yet, what does it mean? When he tries to think of himself and Bibi in a future, away from Mexico or even in Mexico (he has gone so far as imagining himself living the good retired life there), the fantasy doesn't work. Nothing emerges. And the picture he gets of Callie *through* Bibi is frightening—a woman who doesn't actually *do* anything. And he, a man who respects work above all things. Wasn't it the work of holding up the platforms in the Easter procession that had touched him so much?

Besides, Bibi decided this was to be temporary from the beginning. What did she want him for? Bed only? And who said men always used women? It could happen the other way around, that's for sure.

When there are only ten days more to stay—the ten days for which he is paying thirty—John Barnes opens the door to Shauna who appears unannounced.

"I've come for your rent," she says. It is only eight in the morning, but she wears high heels and makeup and a dress with a jacket. She is overwrought or wants him to think so. She swallows hard, flips her hair about, and paces the dining room while he goes to get the check. María stands behind her in the archway, her hands folded, in attendance.

"Really, Shauna, I'm not going to cheat you! I don't have plans to skip town with your valuables," he says. He can't find anything interesting or authentic in the whole place. He hands her the check.

She flushes but doesn't reply, only reads the check as if there is something wrong with it. María waits with downcast eyes, embarrassed.

"By the way, what about my two months security deposit?" Bibi had told him that nobody asked for two months! And at such a high rent!

"You'll get back whatever's left after I've deducted expenses like the phone bill and damages."

"Don't worry. I'm not going to have thousands of dollars worth of phone calls. I've called my publisher once. And I haven't damaged anything."

"I'll return the money to you two or three months after you leave."

"That's not very fair," he says patiently, "to hang me up for so long."

"I have to wait until the bills come in. I'll come by on the ninth to do inventory and check for damages." She pivots and goes out the door.

He stands and watches her walk to the gate. "*Entendió?*" he asks María when Shauna is gone.

She shakes her head no and goes back to work. And so does he, wondering why María is lying. She is smart and surely she understood.

When he next runs into Mel and Linesse, they have their own two children hanging off them as well as net bags of groceries from the street market. They invite him to a birthday party, a combined party for several kids, on the ninth, before he leaves. "You can meet María's children," they say. "And the rest of our gang."

So, his last day will be divided: Shauna in the morning, María and the children in the afternoon, and Bibi in the evening. He will take Bibi out for a nice dinner somewhere.

The ten days speed by as he packs his books, shops for this and that, looks at the bronze-domed cathedral on the hill, and the street vendors and the beggars, as if for the last time again and again. His chest aches to be leaving. How attached he gets to people and things. Even this plastic house he's landed in.

But most of all, María. María. He thinks about her all the time, looks forward to her arrival, regrets her daily departures. He knows her clothing better than he knows Bibi's. He's tried to ask her about her children, about her siblings, about her religious pilgrimages, and she's tried to answer. He's actually tried to explain his book to her! He's said there was sometimes a heart buried under New York's political machine or at least that decisions sometimes addressed human beings with kindness. Did she understand? In their broken Spanish, mostly what's communicated is that he cares about her. And she him? It seems so. They work during the same hours everyday, cheerfully, without complaint. And work is pure.

Sometimes he sits at his desk and just looks at the light coming through the windows and blocks out everything but its bright beauty. He thinks of Callie more and more as a woman from his past, a woman who expected excitement, security, joy, to be handed to her. He wonders if everything that comes to her will seem empty so long as she doesn't do anything to deserve it. He sees now that he loves life far more than she does. He thinks something tricky happened between them. He found her boring without knowing he did. She sensed it and called *him* boring and began to make her way away from him.

Then there are Mel and Linesse raising all those children! How he admires them. *They* aren't bored or boring. He vows to be useful to someone, somewhere, for the rest of his life. In the mean time, he buys small trinkets and toys for the children's party wherever he finds them. When the day comes, he will add a tray of pastries.

The morning of that day comes. It brings Shauna to his door as he knew it would. "Let's be civilized about this," she says.

"Certainly."

She opens a cabinet and using her finger to illustrate her count, counts glasses. "You've broken a wine glass," she says.

"But I bought another set to bring the number up again," he explains.

"One wine glass," she says as she writes it down.

"They were just inexpensive five-and-ten glass!" He almost bursts out laughing, but checks himself.

"And you've cracked the blender cap," she says, going straight to the blender.

This takes him completely by surprise. "I did?" He can't even remember having used the blender.

"Yes." She shows him a hairline crack on the round plastic that connects the jar to the base."

"I didn't realize."

"Well, I did. Or I should say, María did."

Then she skips whole cabinets and goes directly from object to object that she considers damaged. So. She *has* already been here, snooping when he was out. "This wall," she points, has some pen marks from when you wrote the phone list."

"God! You can't even see them!" Now he is really angry.

She moves so fast through the house that he stumbles keeping up with her. María follows behind him, but when they get to a room, she moves past him and stands at attention, her gaze averted. In the section of the bedroom John uses as a study, Shauna points out, "I'll have to get the desk refinished. You've scratched it moving your computer mouse across the wood." In the bathroom, she says, "I'll need yet another toilet seat. You've chipped this one, too, from flipping it up too fast."

"Look, you said you wanted to be civilized about this. What is this really about? You can't be serious about these things."

"Maybe you just don't know how to take care of a house," she retorts. "That's the whole reason for a security deposit." Shauna finds nicks and scratches in her plastic house that he couldn't have known existed. He sees his whole security deposit gone, gone into her wardrobe. And how will he get it back? If he hires a lawyer, it will cost as much as what he's losing.

They go back to the kitchen. "You broke the glass on this table," she says.

"True," he steels himself. He once brought down a pot too hard and cracked the glass. "But I replaced it."

"But you didn't tell me. You didn't tell me. And even though you didn't tell me, I know you broke it. You see," she does another one of her stylish pivots, "María told me. She told me how you took the broken glass to the shop and tried to get the same thickness, but they didn't have it, and you settled on the thinner glass. So you see, I know after all. I have María. She tells me everything." Shauna takes a step backward to get María into her sights.

John has a moment of disorientation. Something flashes very fast, a memory he can't catch, of some moment from childhood. What was it? His grandmother siding with his mother, maybe. To his horror, he loses his years, becomes three again, or four. He feels the blood drain from his face, and his voice takes leave of him. It's not that Shauna is angry, that's not the worst thing. Or that she will take his money. Although that's bad enough. It's that she's claiming María. She's telling him María isn't his at all, but hers.

He tries to look at María, but she looks away still, downward, as if checking the clean floor. Her refusal to look up punches him in the gut, shortens his breath. Shauna says, pushing the list of damages across the table, "Do you agree to these things?"

He rubs a hand over his eyes. "How can I agree to them? You're attacking me for just living."

"If you'll sign this piece of paper," Shauna says. He sees the blur of María out of the side of his vision as he shakes his head no. Yes, she must have reported every little scratch for Shauna to be able to walk in and be so thorough in her castigation. He is a romantic fool not to have noticed that María is only Shauna's employee. And he can't remember chipping or breaking anything except the table glass.

"I'm sorry you feel that way," Shauna says. "I'll leave the list here. You think about it." Then she tells María to look after everything while she is away, and she leaves.

For the rest of the morning, after Shauna is gone, he finds himself tiptoeing about the house. And María tiptoes too. She is quieter than ever. Even when she comes to remind him that she will leave early because of the children's party, she is down to a whisper.

He buys the pastries halfheartedly. But he can't *not* buy the pastries because he's had this idea for presenting them for so long. In the same uncertain and pained way, he hands over the envelope to María that he has had prepared for days. The equivalent of two hundred dollars and a note, which tells her what a pleasure she's been. He can't *not* give it to her. She thanks him quietly twice without opening it and leaves.

Tomorrow, Lynn Stroub, with her wild eyes and spiky hair, will pick him up at six in the morning and spirit him away. He will not see Shauna Walters again. He will leave an unsigned list for her. At least there's that.

The good-bye evening with Bibi is more difficult than he imagined. They are both struck into silence. For entertainment he tells her about Shauna's sweeping tour of the house, and she tells him he should have yelled bloody murder. He feels the sting of criticism in her reaction.

The thing that surprises him is that Bibi cries. All through the night. "Oh, it's just foolishness," she says. "I hate partings." He holds her all through the night, hardly sleeping at all and wondering how he could have thought their ailing relationship would cost them nothing. He's used her after all, let her be a way of saying good-bye to Callie. And then it's over. Five o'clock in the morning comes, and he gives her a final kiss and goes home to check and recheck his bags.

He wonders if María will come at dawn to say good-bye, knows she has thought about it, considered it.

But Lynn Stroub arrives early, packs him into her car. Her eyes look more alert than ever, but she is not in a mood to talk. That's fine. He's not either. He's tired and wants to concentrate on where he's going, to a new life away from Callie and to an as-yet-unknown woman with whom he plans to talk and argue and plan. María doesn't come. But it's all right.

He is all right. The party for the children yesterday was the best time he's had in his five months in Mexico. How happy they were with the pastries and gifts! Oh, he was a hero for bringing them. He drank wine and made conversation with the other adults there, aware, all the time, of the awkward silence that had come between him and María. She hadn't thanked him for the money. He hadn't told her he understood: She had her job to maintain, a life to maintain. He would leave, but she still had to deal with Shauna. He hoped for this exchange, but she was always across the yard, no matter how many times he moved.

All around him, children squealed with excitement, played games, marveled over the hot dogs. They tasted good to John, too. All the children with May and June birthdays opened presents from Linesse and Mel. The toy trucks and balloons and dolls made them so happy. And then the big surprise: A band of musicians arrived!

"How did you do this?" everyone asked Linesse and Mel, meaning 'How can you afford this?'

"Just for once," they said. They still wore the same clothes, the clothes they wore every day, clothes that María washed for them at some interval in the early mornings.

Eventually there was dancing to the Maríachi band. The music was infectious. John wanted badly to dance. Mel and Linesse danced with each other. The rest of the people he didn't know very well. He'd invited Bibi but she hadn't wanted to come. "I don't know. Not to a children's party," she said.

María's little daughter Linda came up to John, tapped him on the leg and ran away. Somebody else pushed him into the circle and he found himself beginning to dance, not with anybody in particular, with everybody. He couldn't explain it, but he felt really happy. When he looked up, there was María, across the yard, nodding to him to go ahead and enjoy himself, nodding encouragement as if she knew him down to the depths. He could still feel where Linda had tapped him on the leg. Surely she'd been sent by María.

THE MAN IN THE BUICK

Fran looks across the breakfast table at the younger of her two sons, Alan, just home from college at the end of his junior year, and something happens to her that reminds her of mercury dipping in a thermometer after a few hard shakes. She feels something drop in her. She loves him so much. To think he is hers, this six-foot-tall man, no longer a boy, a senior in college, with his fine light hair, sleepy eyes, and such a kind look about him. Kind. Yes, he looks a little like her father did. Why does she feel when she looks at him, and he looks back so simply, that she has *lost* something, lost *him*? After this summer, almost certainly his last summer at home, and that's how it *should* be, she will no doubt see even less of him.

Of course. She knows that. Just as she knows that one day she will die. When she hears of people whose children have died before them, she can't imagine it. It would be unbearable. This morning, so full of love, is also filled with vague fears and with this odd dipping feeling, with its ebbing energy, as if by thinking of loss she touches the moment of her own death and separation from all she loves.

"What will you do today?" she asks, proud that she has swallowed the part of her feeling that was jealous of his time. It was hidden, perfectly hidden, as it should be, the mean petty feeling of wanting to hold onto him. She knows he must check in with Joe Benton, his summer boss at the recreation center. He said so last night when he got in.

"I promised Joe the whole day," he says. He sops up the last of his eggs with the last of his English muffin. "I should have said I'd start tomorrow. I could use a day of sleep. But…too bad for me!" He gestures happily, his arms thrown back. "Bad planning." He looks happy. His wide gesture makes Fran laugh. "How about you, Ma?"

"Errands. Food shopping. Other shopping. I'll be going to the mall. So if you can think of anything you need, just tell me."

"Nothing," he says, leaning back in the chair and stretching. "Oh," he changes his mind, "yes I can! Socks. Sports socks. Just sports socks. Nothing to bother about, but if you see them…"

"I'll get them for you." She is glad for this small task, a way to give him something.

"I'll show you what kind." Alan finishes his orange juice, then the rest of his coffee, gesturing to his mother as he swallows to wait just a moment. And then he goes for the sample sock.

She leans back in her own chair, leans against its cushiony high back and closes her eyes. Inside, beams of light splinter and swim away.

"Sleepy?" Alan asks.

"A little."

He shows her the sock. "Like this."

"I remember. I'll try to find them."

"You're the greatest." From behind her, he puts his arms around Fran, chair and all, crossing his arms in an embrace over her shoulders. She reaches up and holds onto his arms for a long moment, kisses them, and then gives them a zip of release with her fingers.

With her older son, Jacob, it always hit her after the fact. The first day of school, oh, that was a bad one, the day he went away to college and two years ago when he said he was taking a job in Seattle. But this feeling, as if life is leaving her body right on the spot—no, she doesn't remember it *quite* like this. Even when Aaron had a mild heart attack, when she drove him to the hospital as he asked, when she sat with him afterwards, stunned as she was by this reminder of his mortality, no, she didn't feel quite the way she feels today. Maybe because they'd talked it out, prepared themselves for losing each other, talked about the fact that one day one or the other of them would have to cope.

Today. She wonders if she is quite well.

She does routine things anyway. While rinsing the breakfast dishes for the dishwasher, she glances over at the calendar on the wall. Aaron's day is jotted in: hospital until nine, office until three-thirty, lawyer four o'clock until question mark, home at six. No star for "on call." She will have his company tonight. Her schedule is down, too: hospital nine to twelve, lunch with her friend Brigit, then an open space for the afternoon. Only a week ago the whole day, every day, was filled with her job. At the high schools she evaluates learning-disabled kids. But now, the days of summer vacation, except for volunteer mornings, have plenty of room.

Sometimes in summers, she runs into Aaron at the hospital. Usually he is leaving as she is arriving. There is something exciting still about seeing each other unexpectedly, for Fran at least. They wave, Fran feels the rise of a blush, they kiss in passing. And she thinks—yes, there is that same feeling or something like, it—no, don't go yet. She often stands at the gate and waits for him to get to his car and drive back past the gate on his way to the office. He waves, amazed, and pleased, too, that she stands waiting for him once more. And then he is gone, and she goes into the wing where she volunteers. She reads and plays games with children, small ones who are there temporarily and who need to be entertained, soothed, or hugged. The other children need care, too, she knows. Someday she will work with the seriously ill. She has been thinking about it.

Alan's long arms go around her again, and she catches a kiss planted somewhere between her cheek and her ear. "See you," he says. "I'm due at eight-thirty."

She turns to see him. She says, "Oh, handsome!" because he looks so nice to her but also because she hasn't had enough chances to *look* at him yet. He laughs, and then she does. She kisses him. "See you." The two of them laugh easily. She can even do it today, although now that she thinks of it, she *woke up* feeling sad, feeling that she'd somehow lost something. She must have had a dream that slipped away.

She'll talk to Aaron tonight as she usually does in the late evenings. She thinks her questions out loud. When the children were younger, she used to wonder, "Am I too easy on them? Do I spoil them?" Lately she has thought perhaps she is too lucky, and it scares her a bit. "Should I work with the children who are dying? Have I had it too easy?" Not that she expects answers from him. She lets him witness her questions.

"Enjoy what's on your plate," he said not long ago.

"But I do. I just want. . . ."

"To be perfect?"

She'd always come in for some teasing of that sort, not just from Aaron. Her neat Italian knits, her hair with the gray ever so slightly jazzed over with burgundy, her poise and serenity. The extra mile. She gave Aaron a nod and a wry smile. "The unexamined life is not worth much. Is that how it goes?"

"Well, darlin'," he said, "yours must be worth a million bucks."

One-thirty: supermarket. Two-thirty: mall. She wrote these in. "So my life is worth a million bucks. In today's market—!" Well, there, at least she's getting her sense of humor back.

As she heads toward the mall, the feeling returns. As if she is losing blood. Something is gone from her, but she doesn't know what. She looks at the highway as if she's never seen it before. No, she hasn't. The signs seem luminous. Busy Beaver. Sears. All kinds of restaurants.

Today they look as they might in a dream, important and vague at the same time. "You're tired." It's Aaron's voice she hears when she needs to tell herself something like that. "Why don't you take a day off? Or two?" But he isn't there to press her. And the part of her consciousness that he owns says nothing else. And then she hears the static on the car radio and realizes that she has been tuned to static since she got into the car. When she shuts it off, she hears road noises and horns somewhere, but they seem to punctuate a great silence.

There is nothing much she has to get except the socks. And they aren't a necessity. The rest of the time she will browse, maybe look for a sale, maybe buy another Father's Day present for Aaron. She has already bought him the books and camera equipment he requested. Maybe a sky-blue shirt like the ones she used to buy her father for every holiday, although what she bought then wasn't as good quality, certainly not as good as what Aaron is used to and what she can afford now. The blue is the thing though, a clean crisp blue, but it must have something sophisticated about it, checks, maybe, or a line to soften it and make it subtle.

And then, in the midst of this thought, she sees something so astounding that she drives into the mall parking lot and just sits there for a moment, not attempting to park. She saw, or thinks she saw, her father, in the old Buick, coming out of the mall parking lot just as she was turning in, he on one ramp, she on another. He saw her. Or at least she thinks so. One hand came away from the steering wheel in a kind of salute to her. No, it was more the look, the look on his face that he'd seen her, calm, but that even though he'd seen her he couldn't stop, he was on the ramp, there were other cars behind he seemed to say in a gesture, and so he couldn't stop although he wished to, and he kept moving.

It isn't possible of course. She knows that. Even though the car, the hair, the mustache, more than that, the look of the eyes, was the same. It isn't possible because he died twenty years ago.   Someone who looks like him, of course. Someone who looks just like him. If only she could just *see* the man again.

The mall lot is not very crowded. And she can park just about anywhere. But she cannot get over what she has seen and in a while finds herself still driving along the access border at the end of the parking space. For some minutes she has been doing this, driving, indecisive, driving around as people do when there are no places to be found. She is not up to shopping. She had better turn around and go home. Yes.

Yet when she leaves the mall, she turns as people so often do, by accident, onto the wrong ramp, the one that goes in the opposite direction from her home. She is not angry about this mistake, nor alarmed. She does not try to figure out where she might turn around to get onto the other ramp. For she knows now that she looked back and that she saw the Buick go this way. And, more than anything, she wants to see this man who almost waved to her and who drove the same old car, white top, green bottom. The same. There is almost no chance he will be on the road, but she has time to spare today, and another glimpse, just another look at him, is all she wants.

Three o'clock traffic. Things are more bottled up than they were before. At a green light of almost ridiculous brevity, only three cars get through. Fran has to sit and wait for the next. She sighs and thinks, "Well, that's it. It's impossible now. I'll just drive on, stop at the next shopping center, buy socks for Alan and go home from there." It'll be even quicker; the main highway links up almost to the shopping center and provides a faster route home than the slow road from the mall. "Yes, that's the ticket," she tells herself, and she hears her father's voice in that expression.

She parks. There are a number of stores here that might have the socks Alan wants, but she'll try Kaufmann's first. She knows this center well because Jacob used to work here during high school and early college summers, at the record store. Now, he's probably given away most of the music he loved then. Probably in a few years he'll be a father, and she and Aaron will be grandparents. She misses him. And in no time Alan will be gone as well.

Kaufmann's has the socks. She asks for eight pairs, handing over her charge. She looks about at the counters and counters of clothes. "Just a minute. I'll be right back," she says to the saleswoman. The blue of a shirt leaps out at her and she goes to look closely at it. But close up, the material doesn't look so good. It has a glaze to it that would make Aaron look as if he belonged in the back room of a bookie joint. Fran takes her time, checking other stacks of shirts. No. Nothing. At least so far as she can see. "Do you have anything else in this blue?"

The saleswoman, who looks sleepy with waiting, is frozen in the position she took when she pushed the pen and charge slip across the counter. "No," she says, but it's not clear whether she has thought about it or not.

Fran, too, is slowed down this afternoon and thinks again that she ought to just go home.

But when she gets back into the car and on the road, she realizes, too late, that she has lost track of her plans and forgotten to take the ramp to the main highway. She finds herself back on the small highway, taking the long way through traffic lights, winding her way back toward the mall again. Which is why when she sees the old Buick once more she knows it is a sign that she must follow it. She sees it way up ahead, turning into the mall. She has a hopeful feeling that by these crazy turns of luck, she will see the man again. And that is all she wants, just to see him. It will be like a time-travel visit with her father, a lovely man, quiet and dignified, steady and just a little mysterious.

She can call up her father very well in her mind's eye—the gray hair, which was thinning, brown eyes encircled twice, first with the darker skin of age, second with spectacles. He had a mustache, small and trim, and he had a jowly face. This is the look she remembers. There is something funny in her memory, though, for she remembers him as he was at the end, and herself, she remembers, at this moment, in a wood-bound yard, just a child, home from school for the summer, spending her day riding a bicycle along a small road that ran along the property or walking around the yard, taking in the luscious smells of lilacs or honeysuckle, finding routines, ways of enjoying the days of childhood. And one of the routines was the way she greeted her father when he came home from the small jewelry store he owned. She'd jump off the bike, run the whole length of the yard and the sidewalk, and throw her arms around him. It was the way he accepted that embrace, understood it, that made it worth doing every day.

A tiny fear that she has not really seen the car, that it has not really entered the mall lot, needles Fran. She drives around the lot again, along the borders looking for the car that belonged to the man who looked like her father. She can't see the car, can't find it anywhere. Up and down the rows she drives, four o'clock flashing on her dashboard, once more around the lot, slowly, even though someone behind her honks and says, "Hey, lady, I'm in a hurry." And finally, not finding it, she parks and walks slowly along the outer border of cars to where she will be parallel with the entrance and then she progresses up the row. And there it is. Not the same white and green Buick. Something like it. A later Chevy. Mostly white with the same forest-green up-holstery. Or is it the same? It is not exactly how she remembers it. Fran squeezes her eyes and looks again. Yes. . .not quite. . .but close.

The mall is not so enormous as some but still large enough that she doesn't know where to begin. Do nothing, she tells herself, do nothing. Just choose a spot in the center somewhere, and if you are to see him you will see him. The center? The best location? She will try downstairs where the concession stands are. The food court is such a small part of the whole mall, but she must do something; walk or sit, each has problems.

Across from her at the Potato Sack she sees that it is 4:45. It occurs to her to change her plan and walk around a bit, but when she goes to stand, it doesn't seem the right thing to do. She might be dreaming about the people she watches while she looks for the man she saw in the car, because as in a dream they move past her steadily and with momentary clarity before they are gone. They are like the signs on the highway, fleeting, memorable: the scowling man who cuffs his son—or is it his grandson?—on the head and neck, who drags him along. How awful the child's life must be. It spreads before her in imagined scenes. No, the boy won't stand a chance.

And mothers and daughters *are* like each other, aren't they? Over and over that is proved. The ages don't matter. The five-year-old and her young mother, the old woman and her very old mother, the teenager and her harried mother. Thank God, her own mother was a good woman. Quiet, kind, competent. Suddenly she misses her. The image that comes to mind is her mother bringing her a bowl of hot soup while she sits looking out at the yard.

People pass. She examines their faces. She sees them better today than people close to them see them. Moles, the style of their glasses, the recentness of a haircut. But when she sees the man she is looking for, it will not be like this, not a close examination, not a matter of moles or glasses. She will just recognize him.

With that thought, she gets up and begins to walk. Into one store, out again, into another. "May I help you?" she is asked many times and she answers over and over again, "No, thank you, just looking around." And they all watch her for a moment because she doesn't look at the shelves or racks at all. And yet she is never treated badly. She commands to-day, as always, a respect. She makes the rounds of the lower level of the mall a second time. "By now he is probably gone," she tells herself. But she needs to feel that she has been thorough. What if he is browsing just behind a shelf and moves when she is asked, "May I help you?" What if when she looks back he's moved to a spot she has just searched? What if she's just missed him?

The steps to the upper level stand before her. She stops for a moment, watches children playing, watches them walk the border and catch the very edges of the fountain spray. Then she climbs stairs.

She comes face to face with a clock. Five minutes until six. How long did she sit downstairs? She must find a phone. Her heart jumps as soon as she turns the corner into the phone bank. There he is, on a phone, his back to her. She freezes and stands there, aware of breathing, just breathing. The man turns. He is not her father. He is not the man in the car. No, not at all, not the right look. He has gray hair and his head is held with pride, but that's all.

She finds a quarter and dials home. Aaron answers on the first ring.

"Hi, sweetheart," he says. "Thought it might be you."

"Time ran away today," she says. "It's six o'clock."

"What's up?"

"Well, nothing. I'm just at the mall, not quite ready to quit yet, and I wondered if you and Alan would mind defrosting some pesto." She stocked the refrigerator today, but nothing is cooked. Oh, surely they can manage.

"Fine with me. I could go for a pizza."

"Don't."

"Or ribs."

"Don't."

"Okay. I'll see what Alan's in the mood for. And I'll have something healthy."

"Thanks."

"Have you eaten?"

"No. Not yet. I may tide myself over with a hot pretzel or something. Save me some of whatever you have."

"Okay. Everything all right?"

Fran wants to tell him that she feels low-spirited today, wants to tell him about the search for the man in the car. But later. She will tell him later. "Yes. I'll be home in an hour or two."

"Good. I mean, it's Alan's first day home. You know how it is. As soon as he contacts a few friends, we'll never see him."

"I'll make it up to him." She can hear a laugh in the background. "What's that?"

Aaron is laughing, too. "He heard me from the kitchen. He told me to quit guilt-tripping him." And then in a tangle of three-way conversation, Aaron speaking more to Alan than to her, they hang up. Fran returns to where she's been, suspended for a day, searching for a glimpse of something she's seen as fleetingly as the last image when coming awake from a dream. She has an imaginary nighttime conversation with Aaron.

"What did the man have on?" he asks.

She thinks. "A blue shirt, a blue striped tie, a light creamy sports jacket, no hat. His hair was gray, thinning in front. Glasses with metal rims, square."

She considers what to do next, sees a bench, empty but for a popcorn box, and decides it's a good place to sit for a moment. She watches people again, calmer this time, having lost the fever of fear that she will miss him. Without thinking, she eats the remains of someone's popcorn. It is easier now. She just waits until she knows what to do, then rises and goes to the end of the mall. She begins to walk the aisles. Maybe he will have left by now. Maybe not. She walks with a slow grace past inquiring salespeople. And as it sometimes happens that a day holds so much of the same thing (people cutting in front of you when you're driving or interruptions from countless strangers whether at the door or on the phone or the answer no, nobody home, nobody able to fix the refrigerator, nobody able to go to lunch), today everyone is kind, solicitous, disappointed when she doesn't require assistance, understanding. Today is a day of regretful smiles and nods.

She has let her thoughts drift. She has covered all of the mall and come finally to the last store. It is just past eight-thirty.

The store is a shoe store. Small. It sells, among other things, sports socks. Some dress shoes, lots of sports shoes.

A woman and her shoeless child sit in two of the chairs. The child, in bright clean white socks, stretches her feet out and wiggles her toes. Just as Fran, having looked about, turns to leave, a man emerges from the inner doorway. She hears him say, "Sorry, we don't have them." She sees him, a glimpse of him, in her peripheral vision, and she turns toward him for a better look. There he is.

At first she does nothing. At first she just stands there and watches him put the child's old sandals back on her feet. He buckles the sandals and squeezes the little girl's toes through them. "Getting big," he says. "Sorry I can't help you," he tells the mother. "They sell very fast in her size."

He doesn't look exactly like her father. But he is the man she has been looking for. And in some way, some way that she can't explain, he *does* look a great deal like him. She takes up a moccasin, turns it over to read the label on the back and turns it over again.

"Is there anything I can help you with?" he asks her. He stands a few feet away from her, holding his hands, clasped lightly, behind his back, and he bows just the slightest bit forward as he asks. He wears a crisp white shirt, long-sleeved, and a red tie with a navy fleur-de-lis pattern. He wears no coat. His pants are of a light gray suit material, perfectly pressed. His hair is thinning just a little. It is gray. He wears glasses of metal with roundish frames. Bifocal lenses. Age, somewhere in his seventies. He must own the shop if he is in his seventies and still working.

"I'd like to look around," Fran says.

"Please do." He smiles, seems tired.

She wants to ask him what kind of car he drives. She wants to ask him what time he came to the mall. But all of that seems unimportant. She's found him after all.

Another mother and child come into the shop. "Is there anything I can help you with?" he asks, bowing slightly and looking from the mother to the child, who is about three.

"I'm looking for a pair of aerobic shoes," the mother says. "For myself. Size seven and a half."

He goes to a table and shows her different styles and colors. "Pink and blue and white," he says. "And this one in khaki green."

The woman points to one of them.

"High tops or low?"

The woman chooses low.

When the customers sit, Fran realizes she would like to sit down, too. She chooses a seat down the row by several from the mother and her child.

"And you?" the shoe store owner asks, turning to Fran. "Can I find you something while I'm back there?"

"Plain white tennis shoes," she says. "Eight and a half medium."

"Right," he smiles. "Right."

The daughter will not stay seated. She picks up every display shoe and examines it. "Jessicaaaa," her mother sings, making the name mean, "put that back," and, "do I have to tell you a million times?"

When the man returns, the child stops moving and stares at him. Fran sees this. The man senses it. He turns to the child. "Hello." He looks as if he might almost say "Jessica," but he doesn't. "And how are you?"

"Fine."

The man turns back to the mother, who is standing heavily on one foot to try out the shoe.

The child flies across the room and throws her arms around his legs. His knees buckle a little. She buries her head in his thighs and doesn't let go.

The mother practically screams, "Jessica!" On her face are horror and embarrassment. Jessica hugs the man even tighter.

"It's all right," he says. "It's all right."

The mother tries to pull her daughter away by tugging at her arm. But her daughter's grip is apparently very secure. "Jessica!" To the man she says, "I'm sorry."

"Jessica," he says quietly. He lifts her, now unresisting, up into his arms. The strain of it, her weight, is hard on him. He lets out a grunt, a look of pain crosses his face, but he adjusts the child until she is comfortable. Which she must be, for she throws her arms around his neck and cradles her head against his.

The mother just looks on, puzzled, distressed. "Jessica," she whispers finally, but the child doesn't respond. "She's never done this before," she says apologetically to the man.

"It's all right," he says kindly. "Isn't it, Jessica? Isn't it?"

It crosses Fran's mind, in words, clear as a ticker tape buzzing through her brain, "This man is ill. This man is dying. This man is going to die soon."

The man very gently disengages the child's arms from his neck. "Oh, Jessica," he says. "What a nice girl you are!" He releases the arms more for the mother's sake than his own.

"I'm sorry," the mother says again, holding firmly to the girl's arm.

The man sees that the mother is distressed, and he nods slightly to show he understands. "It's funny," he says. "It happens to me every day. They come in and they either kick me or they hug me like that. Some really kick. Lots do like Jessica. Some tell me they've seen me on television."

"Really?" The woman appears to think about this. She takes money out to pay for the shoes. "I wonder why."

"Maybe I look like everybody's grandfather." He moves to take the money behind the small counter to his cash register. The child runs after him and embraces his legs from behind. She catches him mid-stride, but he stops and lets her hold him. They pause. Jessica presses her cheek against the back of his thigh. Her mother says nothing, but it is clear she is as horrified as she was the first time. Finally he pats the child's hand and rubs it until she lets go.

Fran believes that she sees the man more clearly than the mother can. He gives something of himself to children, even the children of strangers. He's sad because he's tired. And because he won't live long. She feels she sees right through to him.

Before she knows it, he has turned his attention to her. Before she knows it he has slipped a plain white tennis shoe onto her foot and tied it up. How gently he does everything. What does it matter what kind of car he drives or when he came to the mall?

"My own grandchildren are coming to see me this week," he says.

"From far away?"

"Yes," he nods. "I'm glad I'll get to see them."

"I can understand." When Fran rises, he does, too. She tests the shoe as the other woman did.

"I'll take these," she says. "I think. . . I'd like to wear them." She hands him a twenty dollar bill and watches him make his way behind the counter. She watches him put her other shoes into a bag, tear off a receipt, and make the change of a penny. Time has flown again. Her watch tells her it's closing time.

She drifts behind a sale rack where she can pretend to examine sandals, too-high heels, even turns them over to look at the price. She can see her receipt, a penny, and her sensible low-heeled shoes on the counter. The man who looks like her father takes his glasses off and squeezes his eyes with thumb and forefinger, then puts them back on. She watches him as he stands and waits for her. All around the mall she can hear the sound of security gates rolling, clattering down, crashing to a stop.

Finally she goes to him. She sees a bit of string on his shirt sleeve. "Just a minute," she says. She plucks it off, saying, "There," and slowly smoothes her hand over his arm as if to brush off some remaining particle lingering there, something, some little thing, which might keep him from being perfect.

CHINESE MASSAGE

I

In the morning I took a tour group to see the great caves of Guilin, the ones in which the limestone formations suggested broccoli, cauliflower, cabbage, and other vegetables and fruits. I wanted to tell them, "This is almost art," but they weren't much interested in my theories. They were enchanted by the fact that some of the limestone really looked like a bunch of grapes, that another section was as broccoli-like as it was possible to get. And they were hot. They were dying of the humidity and hundred-degree weather.

We got back to the hotel about noon.

A man named Jim Murdock came up to me just as I was scheduling myself a massage at the hotel desk. His wide smile was strained. Right behind him was his wife Violet. He looked awful. At first he just said he needed to buy a cotton shirt somewhere and could I tell him where to go. I thought everybody knew better than to wear synthetics in the heat, but Violet was a tidy sort who wanted to wash out and hang clothes in hotel rooms.

Murdock's shirt was soaked; his face was wet. New beads of sweat appeared on his forehead as soon as he mopped the old away. Both Murdocks were a little round but very nice-looking. Jim Murdock had an aggressively happy, Howdy-Doody face.

I should have listened to Jim Murdock more closely, but the round-faced girl behind the desk was saying the massage would cost the equivalent of ten dollars American. When I brought out the paper yuan and tried to hand them to her, she seemed angry and bit out, "No. You give doctor. He come to your room. Eleven o'clock."

The Murdocks reminded me of my parents, maybe only because they were the right ages. Or maybe because I'd seen them coming out of the baths in our *ryokan* in Kyoto—the first week of our tour had been spent in Japan—and they'd been pink, wrapped in terry-cloth kimonos, purified-looking, as if they'd undergone something religious, not just a hot bath. And of course, there they were, in what looked like night clothes.

They irritated me, but I was fond of them. I wanted to help them and hoped to be rid of them at the same time. "We've got to find you a cotton shirt," I said to Jim Murdock. "The shops are closed now, but you could buy something at four, even if only a cotton tee shirt. I'll get the bus driver to stop somewhere for you."

Jim Murdock was horrified. He snapped at me, "No, I don't want a tee shirt." He said he'd lie down for a while. So I walked the Murdocks to their room, which was just next to mine. Jim didn't look good at all. I tried to talk to Violet while I watched him. "Weren't the caves fun? This morning?"

"I loved the broccoli and cauliflower," Violet Murdock offered. "I tried to get photographs, but I don't know if they'll come out."

When I got to my room, I sat at the edge of the bed, crushed by the heat and feeling lonely. Lately I'd found myself having imaginary conversations with Dick Cooper, the last lover I'd had. What remained of him in my mind was his irritability.

"Aren't the Dentons unbelievable? What sour people!" he grumbled that afternoon.

I asked him, "Do you think Jim Murdock's seriously ill?"

He said, "Old people like to fuss."

There was a haze in the air. Everything was wet. I slipped into the damp sheets. I lay down and looked at the jug of hot tea water across the room, too tired to get up for it. And besides I wanted a glass of *cool* water, unheard-of in Chinese hotels. Out of the cup, which sat beside the jug, something large and cockroach-like, crawled up and over, and then scampered away. I turned over and tried not to think about it.

After a long time, I fell asleep.

When the Murdocks came to my room and woke me from my nap to tell me they were leaving and wanted their money back, Dick Cooper prompted me to say, "You can't do that. Even if I could get you the money, which I can't, you can't leave China. Not just like that." I was in no position to do a miracle because I was supposed to take everybody on a Li River excursion in an hour. But I went downstairs to make inquiries anyway. The hotel staff told me the Chinese tour guides could manage without me if necessary. I found myself, in spite of Dick Cooper, directing a cab driver to take me to Immigration.

It turned out the Immigration building was only two blocks from the hotel—although nobody bothered to tell me. The cab driver pointed downward to mean that he would wait for me, but I waved him away and entered the square of concrete. Inside, a frightened-looking young man asked me to wait in a large bare room. At the door of the room was another frightened-looking young man with a rifle. Whenever anybody moved or spoke, there was an echo. I felt detached from everything, from time, reason, color. After I'd waited for an hour, resigned that I would miss the Li River trip, I stood, intending to ask what was happening. The young man who guarded the room jumped and raised his gun. I sat down again. After another hour, I was shown to a room where an older man stared at all the papers for a long time. Then he wrote his name, or perhaps it was something else, next to the Murdocks' names on the group visa. He attached two innocuous-looking pieces of paper to their passports.

"Is this all they need to get on the plane?" I asked him.

"No problem," he said slowly and with no levity at all. Could it be that simple?

I walked back to the hotel. All the way the cab driver who had driven me to Immigration followed me. I might have been in a spy movie or a thriller. Dick Cooper appeared finally and began to walk me back to the hotel. I said, "Maybe the cab driver just wants to make sure I'm all right." He laughed like I was an idiot.

The usual sorts of beggars were on the street, mothers with children at their breasts, small children without clothes, old women. I dug into my belt purse and extracted all my coins. I gave them indiscriminately, not to the smallest or oldest or dirtiest but to whoever pressed me hardest.

Dick Cooper's voice said, "You know you shouldn't do that. They'll surround you, they'll swamp you, they'll never leave you alone. And it doesn't really help. That's the thing. Rice one day, starvation for two weeks after. How can your coins help? You are an ant on Mt. Rushmore."

At a street stand, there were bottles of Coca-Cola, and a group of children were drinking some of it from a plastic bag with a straw in it. I wanted a Coke, but the bottles from which it came looked too dirty. The children crowded around me and tugged roughly at my clothes, grabbed at my belt-purse and pockets. "No more," I said. "No more." I wrenched free. The cab driver watched me. Old Dick Cooper was nowhere around.

My dinner was horrible, unidentifiable things drenched in oil. I tried not to think of the food everyone else was having at a cookout on the river boat. The Li River was the most beautiful sight in China, people said. Even the Murdocks, eager to leave China, went. I was the only one from my group in the hotel dining room.

After dinner I wrote a museum check for four hundred dollars and slipped it under the Murdocks' door with their passports and a note. My group hadn't returned yet. It was eight-thirty. I went to my room and lay down.

I dropped into a deep cave of a sleep. I was awakened by the sound of knocking at my door. I could hear it, but I couldn't get up. I felt unbelievably tired, as if I'd been drugged. Finally I struggled up. I held onto my tangled kaftan and stumbled to the door.

"Massage?"

I looked from the man in the hall to my watch. Eleven o'clock. The doctor carried only a towel and a bottle of something. He was bigger, huskier, than most Chinese. He wore thick black-rimmed glasses. When I closed the door, it was suddenly dark except for the natural light of the moon. I started toward the wall switch, which operated a stark overhead light, but the doctor said, "Not necessary."

Then he said, "Take off," indicating my kaftan.

I thought, "Oh, well, he's a doctor," and so I did. He motioned for me to get onto the bed with my head at the bottom. I lay on my stomach, my hands down at my sides, my muscles tense enough for three doctors. The doctor touched my shoulder to indicate that I should turn over. From next door the Murdocks' voices floated in, busy, in contention of some sort. Maybe Violet didn't really want to leave; maybe they always argued when they packed. Surely they were happy about their money. I was risking my job in giving it to them. I tried to hear what they talked about, but I couldn't.

"You're a doctor?" I asked, as the man rubbed solution from the bottle onto his hands and then onto my arm. I imagined the solution was yellow.

He nodded.

"Where did you study?"

"Beijing."

"And that's...?" I pointed to the bottle.

"Oil."

"You work all day and then you do this?"

"Yes."

At first the massage was smooth, just an easy rub of my muscles, but then it changed—his touch becoming deeper and deeper—until it hurt, and I almost yelled out.

"Your name?"

"Dr. Chen."

The Jones of China. Should I ask him to stop? To go lighter? I was about to, but I was just becoming used to it, familiar with the pain.

"Married?"

"No," I said. "No."

Dr. Chen produced an expression of surprised sympathy. My single state here was as bad as if I had lost a leg. He clicked his tongue.

"Someday," I said, "I will." It occurred to me that this Chinese massage was something like Rolfing or what I'd heard of it. When Dr. Chen dug into my belly, as if he were kneading dough, I felt deep, painful sadnesses.

In the hallway outside somebody laughed and somebody else gave a screechy giggle. The Murdocks next door talked less now, were quieter, the words spaced out. Chen's un- believable fingers attacked my neck and shoulder muscles from behind my head. I was still lying on my back. I felt the muscles give up and stretch out, sore.

Two hands appeared over my face, aimed for my breasts. There was something mechanical in their approach. I thought, even in that split second, of Charlie Chaplin in *Modern Times*, the hands unable to stop working on nuts and bolts, the mind registering sex.

"No," I said.

Again, surprise. "No?"

"No."

He came around to look at me to be sure. "No?"

Did other women *insist* on a breast rub? I shook my head.

He shrugged and told me to turn over. I would have thought I'd be less relaxed, more *on guard*, with Dr. Chen after the exchange about my breasts. Yet, moments later, as he massaged my shoulder muscles and my back, I passed over into his control. I might as well have taken several doses of a drug that had just hit. I understood he could do anything he chose to do to me, and I couldn't stop him, simply wasn't able to. I had no volition left, could not initiate, could only react.

From the Murdock's room something sounded strange. *Very* strange. I struggled to hear. The Murdocks were not having a conversation about packing or money. Something else. Chen pressed my buttocks hard.

And then I recognized the sounds from next door. Wasn't it? Yes, it was. The Murdocks were going at it. Jim

Murdock was grunting with the pain of pleasure. He groaned again and again, cried out. I thought, hooray.

But then, I thought, no, something was wrong, wasn't it? The sounds were. . . off? Too frightened, too pained? My God, I thought then, this is a heart attack. It suddenly hit me that Jim Murdock was dying.

I tried to raise up on my elbows, but Chen's fingers worked so fast, that he pushed me down before I ever got up; it was as if he had several of those wooden massage gadgets rolling over my neck and back, legs and buttocks. I felt so many sensations at once, I couldn't tell what part of me he was touching. I said in a panic that I thought Jim Murdock was dying, but Chen didn't seem to hear me. Dick Cooper said with a harsh laugh that Jim Murdock was *living*—coming, not going. I thought, "Can't Chen hear? Doesn't he know there is trouble next door?" I wanted to call out, "I have a doctor here," but somehow I didn't. I just kept listening. The sounds were so awful, Mrs. Murdock's voice coming through, too—a strangled sound—but still I didn't know which it was, I didn't want to be foolish, and I couldn't stop the doctor.

I felt the orgasm coming from a long way off. A long way. The whole time it made its way toward me, I told myself no, I can't have this, not here, not now. I tried to concentrate on the Murdocks, but the sounds were tangled, unfathomable. I tried to concentrate on the doctor. Was he touching me, there, that way? At first I couldn't tell, but it seemed he *wasn't*. He moved all around me, promising to. I found myself thinking, "Touch me," wanting it so badly, "touch me." He didn't. And yet he might have. Might as well have. He made something like air currents sweep over me by the lightning rapid movement of his fingers everywhere but there, and so really, there. The pleasure kept coming at me and in the end it was big enough to quiet my protests and surround me completely. I felt immersed in beauty.

II

One day, a year later, I got into the elevator at the museum, carrying a stack of books, all about China. This was when I met San. He was among the six people riding the elevator. He asked, "You study China?"

"The art, yes. But I'm an amateur." I added, "Of course it's a big subject."

"You go to China," he said, "even better away from book."

"I've been to China."

"Already been!" The many lines of his face went upward in exaggerated amazement. Everybody on the elevator seemed to get a charge out of him. The elevator stopped at the fourth floor and I said, "I have to get off here." San got off the elevator, too; he followed me and told me his name, San Xiou, but that he was known as Alfred by his American friends. He proposed meeting for lunch the next day, just outside the museum.

Right off, I liked his name and refused to call him by his chosen English name. "All right, San. I'll meet you."

We both carried brown bags. We sat on a large marble bench, which faced one of the gardens. It turned out that San had recently finished a degree at the Graduate School of International Affairs and was looking for work.

"Is there work in Pittsburgh?" I asked.

"I try everything. Got translations to do for law firm. Paint houses, too, and contractor work. In one year I will start import business with my friend. He make many arrangements now." From his brown bag he took carrots, a sandwich of white bread and what appeared to be bologna and, later, a plum. I had a piece of chicken, a chunk of cheese and some cut broccoli.

I said, "I expected to see you bring a Tupperware bowl with some wonderful stir-fry over rice."

"Tup-ware?" he asked.

"Plastic."

"Oh. I can cook. I can cook ver well. I can do anything. Everything I do is ver well."

"Oh, I see."

"I can. I will cook you a meal, whatever you like. Anything. Just tell me." He sat forward, all energy. When he smiled, wrinkles formed on every plane of his face, most of them directed upward, clownlike, ready for red and white paint. It was an old face, probably had been from childhood. I found it oddly beautiful because San's eyes were alive with feeling and intelligence.

San told me that even though he was only five-eight and a hundred forty-five pounds, he was very strong. He said he ran every day and exercised his muscles. The last was certainly true. I could see it. He was all sinew. But I knew even before we stood to throw away our lunch bags, that the height and weight he'd given me were lies. I remembered from the elevator meeting that he was shorter than I, which would make him more like five-five. And I guessed he weighed a hundred twenty-five. Just what I wanted to weigh.

We sat down again and talked. I found myself, a well-fed Desdemona, moved by his thinness, a badge of his suffering, one of the effects of the war-service he'd seen.

For years, he had starved, he told me. "I am small because I do not have food. Many years. Could not grow."

"When was this? In childhood?"

"All times. At home, in army. I have to go army when I am thirteen."

A shiver went through me. "What army?"

"Red Guard."

I shook off the shiver. "Didn't they feed you in the army?"

"Not ver much."

"I always thought the army got whatever food there was."

He shook his head. "Terrible experience."

I thought to say something like, "American boys at thirteen wolf down three burgers and guzzle a quart of milk at a sitting," but I realized I would have to explain too many of the words. Talking with him slowed me down.

"In the army...did you kill anyone?"

"No," he answered, not quite looking at me. "I hated army. That was another time. No choice. All young men have to go."

I did not ask him how many precious vases he had smashed, how many paintings he had put into the fire.

He wanted to know why I'd gone to China.

"I take tour groups," I told him. "It's one of our museum programs. I've been three times. I'm going again in a month. Actually six weeks."

He looked sad at this news. "Oh. You will be gone."

"Only for two weeks." What was I to make of him? This child-like old-mannish man who sat there with the heels of his hands pressed against the marble. He wore a navy blue shirt and cocoa-colored trousers, which from the cut, I determined to be at least twenty years old. Both garments were made of polyester, now scratched and bubbled with wear.

"But who will go with you in tour group?" he wanted to know.

"Older people mostly. Retired. Widowers, widows, divorced people. People with enough money and time to take a big trip. I've been twice to Beijing, last year to Guilin and Guanzchou, never to Shanghai."

"I am Shanghai," he said, a hand to his breast. He said his mother lived on a farm nearby and that he sent her money every month. "You go to Shanghai?"

"Yes, this time." Did he want me to make a delivery, I wondered. That was hardly logical since he had already found a way to send money every month. In my mind were poised an image of his mother and the people I generally took to China. A study in contrasts. My people with their jogging shoes and caps with bills, cameras, belt-purses, water jugs. His mother, no doubt, weathered and wrapped in old cloths. "When did you last see her?"

"Four years. First I come to school, and then after Tieneman Square, nobody go back to China. I send her money. She send me letters say, 'Stay away. Don't think of me.'"

"But your brothers and sisters?" He shook his head. "A father?" He shook his head again.

"Only two of us."

"You may never see her again." I couldn't imagine a permanent separation from my parents. "Do you miss her?"

"Of course."

I told him I was forty years old and he told me he was thirty-five. It might have been a lie, like his height and weight. I felt my heart press hard against my chest. I thought at once that I was becoming odd and isolated, a woman who travels extensively and never finds love but that at this moment there was the possibility of love and I shouldn't run away from it.

As I told San things about myself, I saw myself as a stranger might see me—scheduled, blocked from feelings, lonely. I went to China once a year, I explained. I went to work at the museum five days a week. I went to the supermarket every other week and bought meats that could be put straight into the broiler, then also cheeses, fruits, vegetables. I almost always ate alone. I liked my colleagues well enough, but they were a lot older than I and didn't have any time for me. Or perhaps, I thought, I was just unlovable. This was the picture of me that emerged as I answered San's questions. I confessed to him that what I really wanted was to be twenty-five again, to get a second chance. In love, of course. That was the main thing. But that was not what I told San. I explained that I wanted to get a Ph.D. in art history and that I was saving money toward that goal. "But I'm nervous about it. I'm old to go back to school."

"You will have success," he said, with the bland assurance of a fortune cookie.

I told him I had decided to think of him as a seer.

He shrugged bashfully. "Tomorrow," he said, "I will come to you, cook dinner."

"What should I buy?"

"Nothing. What do you have?"

"Chicken, carrots, celery, lettuce, cheese, wheat bread," I rattled off.

He nodded. "Onions, peanuts, rice?"

"Not peanuts. But tomatoes. Can you do anything with tomatoes?"

"Of course. I can cook with anything. I can cook with nothing."

I found myself standing back while he took over in my kitchen. He put the chicken together with some peanuts and hot peppers he'd brought, the tomatoes and celery with some sprouts he'd brought, the carrots and onions with ginger. The smells were wonderful and I rushed to set the table, putting back the linen place mats in favor of some Pier One specials in black. Simple white plates and the food arriving in whatever bowls San found in the kitchen. As he sat down I fetched chopsticks I'd brought back from China. San was delighted. And *amused*, too, as I used them. The chopsticks, like the problem of finding the right words—the ones he would know—slowed me down.

"This is delicious."

"Of course."

"You know you really shouldn't say, 'Of course,' to everything," I told him. "It's not. . . *polite*. It suggests the other person is *stupid*." I hurried to eat a carrot before it fell from its perch on the crossed sticks.

He looked upset. "Really?"

"Where did you learn it?"

"In book of English conversation."

"Well, you overdo it. You say it too much. Sometimes you should say, 'Yes.' Sometimes, if you receive a compliment, like when I told you the food was delicious, you should say, 'Thank you.'"

"I don't want to be rude," he said with a smile that could wipe away much greater offenses.

San moved, ate, cleaned up the kitchen, did everything at high speed. I told him, "My next trip will include three cities in Japan as well as Shanghai. That's how the museum attracts people for these trips, by giving them many places in two weeks. I like Japan, but I like China better."

"Shanghai!" he said, drying a frying pan. "I am Shanghai."

I told him I knew, I remembered.

He told me, as we stood doing dishes, that I was beautiful.

I didn't know what to say. Wasn't he supposed to prize thin, quiet women with straight black hair? Or their opposites—shapely, unquiet American blondes? I am more the background figure of an Italian painting, the fuzzy-haired friendly saint, round-hipped, thoughtful-looking, secondary to the Madonna or the main saints.

Eventually he sat beside me on the couch, in much the same spatial arrangement we'd had on the slab of marble, a foot away from each other, him in the driver's seat. "I always like woman like you with good face and healthy. And with ambition to learn. In China only meet one woman like this. Dentist. She did not love me. Ver ambi-tion."

"Ambitious."

"Thank you."

"Of course. Just joking. What happened to her?"

"She married other man who is professor now."

"But there must have been other women?"

"I don't like them enough."

I was put off by his mustard-yellow shirt, old and, like his other clothes, of inferior synthetic material. His jeans were not really denim but some odd brushed material with bell-bottoms. I noticed his sneakers were plastic. I tried to see beyond these things, ashamed that they bothered me. I thought, if ever I am to find love, I must change, adapt, compromise.

He leaned over and took my hand.

"Years go by and I am still virgin," he said.

I stared at his green argyle socks, his plastic sneakers. "Please don't rush me," I said. "I have this trip to prepare for. I have so little *time*."

I accepted an invitation to lunch at San's apartment one Saturday. He made small turnovers with something purple and fruity in them, rice, and chicken with sesame. Because San had himself never been to Guilin, I showed him, while we ate, photographs of the Reed Pipe and Seven Star Caves. I told him, "This is almost art." I theorized that the work was done by nature for centuries and urged along by a person who, like an elf, entered the caves secretly and gave nature a little help here and there. Someone surely made the limestone more broccoli-like, more like a bunch of carrots or a head of cabbage.

"No, I think all natural," he said.

"Impossible." That rain and time could make the perfect cabbages and carrots! "Isn't it?"

He shrugged, smiled, and studied the remaining photos of Guilin.

I pointed to a man in a group photograph. "That man, Jim Murdock, was on my trip last time. He had a very hard time with the heat in Guilin. He almost died one night."

"South China is ver hot."

"I didn't do anything, that's the awful thing."

San went on studying photographs. He identified Jim Murdock in another photograph with his wife. He gave Murdock and photographs of the scenery equal, considerable respect.

"Isn't it astounding?" I pointed out, how the *inside* of the cave is a miniature of the landscape *outside* the cave. Nature imitates nature, you know, as the flower of a plant imitates the leaves."

"You will be ver good professor," he said. He stood to clear the plates.

"Let me help?"

"Go, look at apartment," he said proudly.

His roommates, Americans apparently from the way he'd described them, were out. And yet the place bore San's mark and was a touch of China in America: a rickety wooden table with some sort of oilcloth over it, bowls of fruit and vegetables sitting out, the smell of onions and garlic and ginger. Other things. Old furniture. The ways shelves were used for clothes. His bed which looked like a pallet on the floor.

San came up behind me at the bedroom door and said, "Lie down and I will give you massage."

"This is incredible," I said, "that you should offer such a thing."

"Why in-cre-dible?"

"It just is." I told myself that even though I liked fine things—vases, paintings, clothes, and expensive foods; even though I liked to go to the opera and the ballet; liked dates, American-style—that San and I should make a go of it. I heard him say he would one day want to live in China, but I lay down and forced myself to ignore that. I let him press into my shoulder muscles.

"I will pack photographs, a small package clothing, and money envelope. Okay? I will write everything you need to find village of my mother. Okay?"

I nodded yes. "Will I have to leave my group for long, an afternoon?"

"Yes. Pretty far out of town. Okay?"

"Okay."

"You should take off clothes," he said.

"Oh. All right." I felt him tremble as he helped me remove my blouse and then my skirt. When I took off my underwear, he looked away.

"After massage," he said, "take nap. Wake up, have tea."

"All right."

He took his clothes off and lay down beside me. We made love, hastily and nervously. San was elated and kept burying his head in my shoulder and telling me he loved me. I told him it wasn't love, but he insisted it was.

Later, in the kitchen, I told him, "I hope it's easier to hire a car in Shanghai than it was in Guilin. The cab driver really took me for a ride. Oh, in America we say that to mean he cheated me."

"How?" San pretended to be preoccupied with choosing two cups. I watched him. He was wearing a white shirt and black pants. He looked formal, a little like a waiter.

Consulting my watch, I saw that it was four in the afternoon. I said, "I really should get going."

"Today is Saturday. No work on Saturday. Stay and relax. Take nap. Afterwards more massage."

How sleepy it was there. "Maybe."

"Tell me about cab driver."

"It turned out the Immigration building was only two blocks from the hotel. The cab driver charged me something enormous. I can't remember now how much but it was way out of line, high for China. Then he wanted to wait for the return trip!"

"Could have walked."

"Sure."

San shook his head in wonder. "An-gel-a," he said, in a way that made me feel rare. It seemed impossible that I could make anyone that happy.

He cut an apple on a board at the sink and put the pieces on a chipped blue plate. He put it between us on the table. I took a piece while he filled the teapot and brought it to the table.

"Take tea. Lie down. Read, maybe. I will do dishes and when you wake up maybe go for walk."

I surprised myself by nodding. I left him and went back to what I thought of as a pallet but was a perfectly good single bed mattress on the floor. The tattered chenille bedspread was still folded over double, but it was all tossed and wrinkled now. I straightened it and lay down.

Everything was quiet. Almost quiet. I could hear the muffled clunk of dishes and pots being caught by a dish towel before they fully bumped the sink.

When Dr. Chen switched on the light that night, a year before, I saw him fully for the first time. His body inclined inward in apology, but his eyes were angry.

As the time for the trip drew near, I ended up seeing more and more of San. He brought me a map from the library and traced it on thin paper. He wrote directions for a cab driver in Chinese on plain white paper. "Will be surprised to leave city, but will understand after read this. Won't take you for ride," he laughed. He brought several photographs of himself and of places—his apartment and various university buildings. In the photographs he had his arms around American buddies and international friends. He described each of them fondly and told of times he cooked for them. I suggested he write these stories in a letter to his mother, and he did.

One night I insisted we go to a movie; he agreed, reluctantly. He grumbled that he usually watched what his roommates rented on videotape. I offered to pay his way, but he insisted he didn't want that, didn't mean that. So I drove and we went dutch to the Playhouse, which showed old films for $2.00.

They were showing *Broadcast News*. San sat slumped away from me with his face in his hands. I felt awful about pressuring him to go on a date. But what about my life? Was I to sit home all the time, massage my only entertainment?

We had made love two or three times after that first time, but San always initiated lovemaking by offering a massage.

On the way home, I asked him what he thought of the film. I saw that he sat slumped in the passenger seat.

"Excellent film. I saw before, but I don't like."

"You saw it before? Why didn't you say?"

"Is all right. Is excellent."

"Why don't you like it then?"

"Wrong ending. Woman was ver wrong to *inter-rupt* connection between her and man."

"The anchorman? But he turned out to be a fake."

"All people are fake. All men are little bit bad. Women too. Wrong to *inter-rupt* what is already started."

This comment silenced things for some time. In a mood to drive in the wedge I'd put between us, I asked, "Want to go to Gullifty's for dessert?"

"If you want," he said glumly. "I don't want anything."

"Never mind then."

But I couldn't leave it alone. "Why don't we go out to eat sometime next week? We never have. I'll be busy packing, and I won't want to cook. I'll treat you."

"I don't like to go out to eat," he said. He smiled sheepishly and told me, "Someone from my country maybe report me. Then I can never go back."

"Oh. Does that kind of thing happen?"

"Never can tell."

When I pulled up in front of his house, he surprised me further by grabbing me roughly and trying to kiss me. I pulled away. The date *itself* had interrupted something.

"You will have other man in your life soon," he said angrily. "And me. I will be nothing to you."

"What makes you say that?" I asked. Secretly or perhaps not so secretly, I wanted him to be right about this.

"You have ambition. You go graduate school. Meet some man, become professor." San's face, for the first time, was not wonderful to look at.

I shut off the car engine and followed him into his apartment for the packet, which I would take to his mother. There were five days before I left, but I suspected, and I was right, that I would not see San again in that time. When I

returned from China, I found a note telling me he had gone to
live in L. A.

III

I sit in the lunch room of the art building with my two
new friends from graduate school, and I tell them stories of
my trips to China. We are talking about the things that
motivate us to make changes in our lives. And of course we
ache about our classes.

There is Jan, older than I, married with three children, but
separated and on her way to a divorce. Ming, slender, an age-
less thirty, married with no children.

I tell them about my trips to China, Murdock, and about
San.

Ming taps the table. "I want the name of that hotel," she
says. "The name of that doctor." We laugh, but she taps the
table again and insists, "I want to take a vacation."

Jan, more fixed on domestic arrangements, asks about my
most recent trip. She wants to know if I took San's things to
his mother in China.

"I did. The cab ride was a stop and start affair with me
taking out San's letter at intervals and nodding at the driver
and him nodding at me. I found San's mother. She was very
old and sad. Everything around her was. . .dry, dusty."

Ming, who wears a miniskirt, a silk blouse, and a
contemporary haircut, nods.

And I remember, but don't say, the beds were pallets.
That a single skinny chicken trotted back and forth in front of
the house San's mother lived in. Or that even though everything was poor and depressing, I felt comfortable with the old
woman because San's voice had replaced Dick Cooper's and
because he talked to me all the time. He'd say, with some
humor, things like, "That chicken will not taste ver good,"
and "Watch out cab driver not leave you there. Then what?"

"Did you stay long?" Jan asks me.

"No. An hour or so. Some of the other people in her
commune came to stare at me. She made me a cup of tea."

"Did you see what he sent her?" Ming wants to know.

"Yes, because she opened it right there in front of me.
There was money and some clothing and photographs. We

looked at the photographs together. She called to the other women and showed them the pictures. She said something to them. I think she told them what a happy life he had in America. I think she told them I was his girlfriend. I let her think what she wanted."

"San was not for you," Ming says. "Too humble. You should have a man who is equal with you."

My friends tell stories, too.

Jan is divorcing her husband and some days we listen to stories of the fits he throws because she's going to graduate school. What does she want with a Ph.D., he fumes. Ming is happily married, but she's looking for trouble. She's been reading about women who have extramarital affairs, and she finds the prospect fascinating. I can't guess what's going to happen to her. And Ming has ancient matchmaker blood in her, I think, for she is always talking about fixing me up with someone. A dinner, a party, a seemingly happenstance meeting at lunch.

I've found out San's address and written him to tell him he meant a lot to me. I thanked him for intersecting with my life and turning me on the road to happiness, preparing me for newness. I said my friends give me credit for changing my life, but I feel a lot of the credit goes to him.

Oh, and I told San about the Chinese landscapes I'm studying, which some critics think are threatening and negative. Why? Because at first you can't see with the naked eye the little dots that are *people* hidden in the waterfalls and mountains. Isn't there a dark meaning, the critics say, in the smallness of the human, the largeness of the world? But it makes me joyful to see the way vital little people are tucked into the big picture. I told San I understand what the critics are feeling, but I can't agree.

FLIGHT

He'd always gone up and away, she stayed on the ground and that was the way it worked, had worked for twenty-five years. And now Pam could hear him in the bedroom, the familiar scrape of the hangers as he took out his uniform and two clean shirts, the sound of the faucet and, this time, small new sounds that only she, knowing him as she did, would notice.

Of all things to say, that he didn't feel loved, hadn't felt loved by her, ever. "Ever?" she'd asked, so sure that the way she said it, the upturned nose of the question would point out the ridiculousness of the statement.

"No," he'd said. "For the first couple of years I didn't think about it. Then in the third year, I realized that I wasn't loved. And I knew that I was married to the wrong woman." It wasn't the first time he'd told her the marriage was not working for him, but he'd never before said it like that and never said he was leaving for good.

Pam grasped at a thought. He always said "fantastic" or "disaster" to describe a workday or a television program; he was given to daily casual overstatement as a matter of course. Even though she was shaking with fear, even though her thinking was blurred by a rising anger, she moved about as if only a continued conversation was necessary to mend the tear in their lives. "But I do love you," she'd said. "I've loved you for twenty-five years."

"Oh, Pam," he'd sighed.

"Well, just because you can't feel it. . . ."

"I have to try it on my own. A new life."

She brewed a pot of coffee. It was seven in the evening. Since she and Robert never made coffee at night, the smell reminded her of morning. "We live in Newport," she said to herself. "It's seven in the evening. It's beautiful here. I am in my home, which I love. If I open the window, I can smell the ocean breezes."

She could hear drawers being opened and shut in the bedroom. And she was able to identify one of the new sounds as that of a box being pulled across the floor. At the door of the bedroom she found herself knocking, and furious with herself, hearing no reply, she opened it. Robert sat on the edge of the bed, two cardboard boxes on the floor before him, the red canvas bag on the bed where she'd seen it so many times before.

"I have a bag which hasn't been unpacked for twenty-five years," he told people happily. "I'm always ready to go."

And that was the problem, his readiness to go, his need to go, not something she failed to do to make him feel loved. The red bag seemed innocent because it was familiar, but the boxes, with their jumble of books and clothing, pictures of the children sticking up out of it all, were different and terrifying.

"Don't go," she said. "Don't do this. Talk to me."

"What can I say?"

"Tell me what you're thinking. Let's sit on the deck. Let's have a cup of coffee and let's talk."

He rolled his arm slightly to look at his watch. "Okay."

"Okay," she said to herself as if this was something good, this concession, "okay."

How had he known to choose this weekend when Jeannie, their youngest, their wildest and most hot-tempered, was on an overnight at Pam's mother's house? Who had suggested it? She couldn't even remember that. Jeannie hadn't wanted to go, for it wasn't a high-schoolish thing to do, and there was always something exciting going on with her friends. The other children were gone, had been gone off to college, and Jeannie's forceful, bitter-tongued presence had kept Pam and Robert too busy to be alone with each other as they were now on the deck with the coffee before them.

It was hard to sit there with him, to see he looked at her with pity. Pam couldn't think how to start. But then she just did. "Have you thought about how even a small separation is a huge thing, something we can't repair easily?" But she knew he had. He'd mentioned separating in one form or another for years now. And the number of trips he made that were not connected with work, the number of flights to see friends or property in California or Illinois or Montana, had increased steadily over the last few years.

"Yes, I've really thought about it." He looked calm, although he was never calm, had always been in a hurry. For once, his long, thin frame of a body found a balanced position in the chair and his hair, wet still from the shower, fell more evenly forward than usual. Perhaps he would push it to one side again as it dried. The blueness of his shirt and the sweater of darker blue that he pulled over it put his eyes into a perspective of blues so that they didn't shine as alarmingly as they often did.

"Why now? Have you gotten involved with someone else?" She put her hands around the coffee cup, looking for warmth.

"No. No, I haven't."

She drank some coffee, but Robert didn't touch his. "Would you like me to warm it?" she asked "Would you like something to eat?"

"No. Nothing."

It wasn't as if he hadn't been gone before for long periods. The kids thought of him as gone already.

"I've written to Jeannie," he said. "And I'll call her. I wish she weren't so tough," he said regretfully. "I'll talk it through with her. Although she may already know and accept it. Wendy did. She brought it up to me. She said she knew I'd leave, she could see it."

"Wendy said that?"

"Last Christmas. When we went shopping together." He almost laughed. "I don't know where she came from, where she got so strong. She told me I was a jerk."

The companionship of her absent, strong daughter snapped Pam to consciousness. "You are," she said. She felt her eyes turn mean, but he went on, unburned by them.

"But Mark," he said. "I'm worried about Mark. I've talked to him, too. He just shrugs. About everything. He has no plans. He doesn't care about anything."

"Maybe he got that from you." But it wasn't even true. Their personalities were nothing alike. Now, Robert was unlike even himself, sitting still and speaking little except to deal the children like cards on the table between them, their personalities a reminder of the three phases of the marriage. If his hair would fall to one side, if he would move, if he would just talk and talk the way he usually did, he would be back to himself again.

"The children. They won't be all right," she said. And with that, the tears finally began.

Robert stood and pulled her to him. "I'm sorry," he said as he held her tight, maybe tighter than ever, certainly with an awareness of her she'd been missing for years. Her arms went around his waist, tentative at first, but when he didn't pull away, in a desperate tightness to keep him there, at home, forever.

As she held on, she saw far in the distance the speck of a moving figure walking toward the beach. The night was turning dark with the promise of rain and yet someone was moving doggedly to the beach. She felt she *was* that person while she hung onto Robert and while she told herself once more he could not, would not, really leave.

"You've always been wonderful with the children," he said. "With them, you've always been one hundred percent."

An hour later, the boxes and the forever-packed bag were gone. He'd always flown for three days and returned home, except when he went off on another trip on the off-days.

On Sunday and Monday he called several times to talk to Jeannie.

A week, two weeks, a month, and then six weeks went by and he did not return home.

Pam often lay on the bed, letting images drift over her. She remade her life, said things she hadn't said and did things she hadn't done. There had been the question of this house in Newport, which she wanted, had always wanted, New England and the beach being her idea of perfection. And he'd wanted to live in mountainous countryside, an idea she'd dismissed. The property he'd bought for their retreat and the ugly little cabin he'd built on it, practically a child's playhouse, he'd loved in a way she couldn't understand. She should have found a way to enjoy it, to fix it up maybe, instead of refusing to go there with him. She tried to imagine why living for a weekend with kerosene lamps and log-fire heat was restful. It was more simple, she understood, more private, more away from the world. It was his need to be away from the world and from comfort that frightened her.

She should have gone to Colorado when he asked, and Nevada when he did his long drive through the state, and Arizona when he went to see friends there and asked her to go. It wasn't those places, though, that bothered her. Again it was the *need* to go somewhere every weekend. She'd known that Robert entertained thoughts of moving, that he'd hoped to pry her away from her beach and persuade her to live somewhere else. For what? To leave her there?

How he'd leaned toward her as if he were asking for a date when he said, "I love the deserts and the mountains. Please come see them with me." She had gone once, and, although she had to admit it was all beautiful, she felt like an abandoned Easterner looking about for the coziness of walls. Everything was far away from everything else.

Now, though, if she got the chance, she would offer to go with him as often as he liked, until he got it out of his system, this obsession with other places.

"I'd like to come get some things," he said in a phone call about two months after he left. "And to have some time with Jeannie."

"Perhaps," Pam thought, "I can get him to stay for a few days. If only we could talk."

But it seemed all kinds of things had changed. He was soon going to live in Arizona for good, he said. And now, suddenly, there *was* another woman. Who would believe in the convenient suddenness of the new woman? He must have been lying all along. In the deepest part of her Pam knew she had to give up, and yet she couldn't. She could have left the house, but she made dinner instead and tried to stop the argument between Robert and Jeannie, which left them all finally with a heightened sense of silence.

He seemed incredibly tired. He'd never been so still. He lay on the living room floor with his pilot's uniform on still, lay on the border of the Turkish rug they'd bought twenty-five years ago and which she loved so much she'd decorated a whole house around it. Pam sat on the couch and looked at him, saw that a part of him wanted to give up and stay where things were familiar. Before dinner, she'd asked about the woman. "She was there before you left, wasn't she?" But he'd said no, the truth was, honest to God, that he'd met her two weeks after leaving. And he hoped that Pam would meet somebody, too, somebody wonderful, somebody who loved her better than he ever did. Pam saw that although a part of him wanted to stay, mostly he was already gone, already far away.

The first thing Marina thought when she saw the pilot at a party was, "One day I'll be married to that man." She was thirty-three and she'd never been struck by such a clear-cut certainty before. When it hit her, it wasn't a bad thought or a good thought; it was just there. Moments later, friends, who referred to him as the pilot-poet, introduced her to him. They'd whispered excitedly as he crossed the room that he was divorced and wanted to meet women. He gestured wildly and talked at a rapid rate. His clothes pulled and wrinkled as if he'd left them two miles behind him, and his eyes glinted with fervor. Could he really be that interested in baseball, films, poetry, and all the other topics he lighted upon, or was there something else, just a need to be in ecstasy? Marina suggested they meet for dinner and talk some more. Or at the very least, she thought, he could buzz around her again and burn up the air while she listened.

He fell eagerly toward her in the restaurant. "I've been here for two hours," he said breathlessly. "I got here early, so I did bar-talk with strangers. I've been drinking Scotch."

It turned out the information given by her friends was all wrong, as Marina learned over dinner. Robert was not actually divorced from the woman with whom he'd spent twenty-five depressed years, although he *was* planning to be. She learned, too, that he was now deeply involved with a married woman whom he'd met only two weeks after leaving his wife, a woman he despaired of stealing away from her present marriage, a woman who had the virtues of crying a great deal and wearing passion on her sleeves.

Marina felt a distinct disappointment. Why had he come to dinner? Why did he hold her attention with such long gazes? Why—here it was—did she stay, ignoring the facts of his story or at best altering them to suit a more hopeful encounter between them?

Without being asked, Marina told him about her work, how she'd started out as a painter but now did theatre costume design. She explained that she'd just won a citation for *The Rivals* and would soon start on *Arms and the Man*. He appeared to like what she did without wanting to know any more about it.

"Have you ever lived away and apart from things?" he asked. He told her about the mountain cabin he'd built, log heat, kerosene lamps.

Well, actually she had. "My California days," she explained. "I had a friend, the friend had a cabin, the cabin had mice and was surrounded by rattlesnakes."

"And you went there?" He was distinctly joyful. "You stayed?"

"Yes. And I got used to the rattlers, I got rid of the mice, and I got used to myself, actually, to being alone."

"Have you been to Colorado? Arizona?" he asked. "Would you like to live there?"

"I don't know," Marina shrugged. What a lot he had to learn about people and compromise and negotiation and compatibility. He wanted to pack a woman up like a bag and take her with him. On that evening, Marina just wanted to go home. "We've taken up this table for a long time," she said.

"Please stay," he implored. "Let's be friends. Let's talk. Let's talk often. Have brandy or whatever you'd like. I'll leave a big tip."

"Well, all right, a brandy, then."

He had told her over brandy that he had made plans for just about every weekend for over a month. Since he could fly anywhere he wanted, he was visiting friends all over the place. Marina was curious. "What about your friend? The woman you're involved with?"

"When she can get free for a day, I'll fly back."

"That doesn't sound good," she said.

"*I can't* just sit around," he explained. He repeated the same phrase one night on the phone when he called from Denver. Then, "*I can't.* Some people are afraid to move. I'm afraid not to."

"If you were living," Marina said coolly, "you wouldn't be so afraid of dying."

"Maybe not, but that's how it is. Anyway, I'm gone until Wednesday. I'll call you then."

"I'm on pins and needles."

"What?"

"Costumer's joke." Still, Marina had a vague fear for him, that by just being "gone" he was in danger of flying into nowhere. She had a persistent image of the electrical contraptions kept on the borders of swimming pools to kill flies and mosquitoes. In her imagination, the earth's borders were ringed with something like them to keep the inhabitants within the boundaries. "Where will you be?" she asked before hanging up.

"Where will I be?" he hummed. "Let me see."

In the background Marina heard a shuffle, then silence, then a crackle of paper. "Pittsburgh, Roanoke, Pittsburgh, Boston, Hartford, Boston, Pittsburgh, Detroit. Next day: Detroit, Chicago, Philadelphia, Pittsburgh, Chicago, Philadelphia. I asked for Myrtle Beach, but I didn't get it. . . ."

"When you do, look at the ocean for me."

"You miss it?"

"Mmmmmm. I was named for it and it was apt. I'm not sure how I got myself land-bound." She wished she could take her vacation right away instead of waiting until the end of the summer. She thought, without wanting to think it, that Robert would possibly go with her. The flutter in her stomach warned her she was in dangerous territory.

"If I go," he said, "I'll bring you back some sand." Paper rustled again. "Then Philadelphia, Charlottesville, Cleveland, Detroit, Boston, New Haven, New York, Philadelphia, Pittsburgh. Then I'll call you. In Boston, I'm having lunch with my sister. In Philadelphia, I'll rent a car and go visit my cousin."

"You never stop."

"Except in Detroit. Nothing much in Detroit. Just a movie and bed."

Detroit sounded fine to her.

He returned with stories of the unhappinesses of women. Marina heard the stories by late night phone, the vistas of their lives laid out before her in clear outline. She tried to draw while she talked to him, but couldn't really. Later, she tried to finish the preliminary sketches for *Arms and the Man*. She added only a line here and there, but the oddest thing happened. The stout matriarch, Catherine Petkoff, became for the moment Robert's Philadelphia cousin, gratingly cheerful through divorce, money problems, difficult children, and a newly revealed history of childhood suffering. "I don't know what she hangs onto," Robert had said. "How do people get along with so little?"

"How do people in the third world face the next day?" she'd asked.

"I'll have to digest that," he'd said.

But if he did, it would happen some time later, for he went on to tell about the stewardess who'd been through Rolfing, meditation, trans-channeling, and Forum. "She says I need all of them. Every time we have a flight together, she tries to sell me on something. She's bright and cheerful, I have to give her that. But I think she's headed for trouble." Marina found the stewardess in the Raina sketch, full of insistent youth, adorable and false.

And Louka, the fiery, embittered servant, transformed as the pencil made its way across her face, into Robert's sister. "All her life, my mother told her she wasn't pretty, that she wasn't charming, that she wasn't satisfactory. And she wasn't. In that atmosphere, she wasn't. Now she's mature and competent"—she was an insurance executive—"and she *is* beautiful. She *is* now. But she still doesn't know it. She can't believe it. She still ditches the good guys and takes up with the bad guys."

Marina blinked her eyes hard to stay awake. Just another fifteen minutes. The last couple of lines to the men, a trio in the center of the sketch pad. The foolish and lovable Major Petkoff, a fond, overly doting father; Sergius Saranoff with his nose in the air, a Byronic dreamer; Bluntschli, the hero, a reverse romantic with the unnerving power of disarming. Their uniforms didn't look particularly Bulgarian, Marina thought. They evoked airplanes, not mud and cannons. And why were the men clumped together, the women turned and looking at them as if for guidance? She closed the sketch pad with a slap and went to bed.

Once he asked her if he could come to dinner. It was all right except that she caught herself being charmed by the fact that he whistled at the front door as he waited for her to answer it. "My doorbell doesn't work," she said, adding foolishly, "so I have to have good ears." She wiped her hands on a well-loved apron that said, "Feast with the best and welcome to my house." She kept smoothing it down. "It's my *Taming of the Shrew* apron," she added, confusing herself further.

By the second time he came to dinner, it was clear from his eyes that he intended to redefine the bounds of the friendship. "I drove eighty miles an hour to get here," he said. "I went five hundred miles an hour before that. I need to slow down." He had his cap in one hand, his forever-bag in the other. "Mind if I change clothes?"

"Have a shower if you'd like," she said. As she set the table, she heard the altogether unfamiliar sound of the faucet and shower, of him moving around in her bedroom. When he emerged with his hair wet and stuck to one side, she noticed the way he walked. He was extremely tall, and his neck stretched up in a way most tall people's didn't, an attempt, Marina decided, to get his perfectly good head into the clouds. She served plain old spaghetti, but he seemed to think it was good.

"I have to live out West," he said. "That's a certainty. That's the one thing I know."

"One thing? Poor man."

"Other things, too. I can't ever go back to Pam. That's for sure."

The other woman didn't have a name as yet in their conversation, and he didn't mention her. He helped to clear the plates. "Thank you. I feel terrific," he said. "I feel very good."

"Had enough to eat?"

"Oh, yes. Fantastic."

"Coffee?"

"Sure. Coffee."

By the time she came into the living room with the coffee, he had taken the invitation to choose a record and he lay comfortably on the floor while Carmen McRae sang. As she put the tray on one of the small tables, she felt grateful that she was tall, strong, and not easily budged. "Have you got pictures of your children?" she asked. "I'd like to see them."

He rolled over on one hip to get the wallet out of his pocket, and once he had, he pulled out a stack of photographs, which he shuffled like cards. The first thing he showed her was a picture of a truck, a shiny and carefully maintained relic sitting in the dust. "I keep it in Colorado," he said. "She's old, but she's a beauty. Runs well."

"Lovely," Marina said. "She's your horse, isn't she?"

Surprised, then grateful, Robert said, "Yes."

"Does she have a name?"

"Hedy Lamarr."

"Just like Bob Newhart," Marina mused. "I saw a program where he wanted to be a cowboy, had to go out West. You do want to be a cowboy, don't you?"

"I guess so. I keep a hat and boots in the truck."

"Bob Newhart had a ten gallon hat and a studded shirt and riding pants and a very small bag. He said, 'I travel easy.'"

"I don't have a studded shirt."

"That could be fixed." Even though Robert looked uncomfortable as he sat up to drink coffee, even though she could see Gary Cooper pain in his face, she forged ahead. "Bob Newhart was the wimp of the bunkhouse," she explained, "until he took on the bully. The bully was just a crude sort of guy. Bob Newhart just kept telling him off, telling the truth; the truth was his weapon, and that made him a hero. Then he was free to pack up his costume and go home."

"He's a funny guy."

"To Vermont in his case. They're re-running all those old shows. I'll tape it for you if it comes on."

"Good," he said, his face registering a mind ticking away. "Well, here they are," he announced, proffering the pictures of his children. "Wendy. Mark. Jeannie."

He told all about each one, but Marina concentrated on the *looks* of the photographs: happy and strong, sullen and sulking, angry and mean. "She must give you a run for your money," she said, pointing to Jeannie.

"Whooo," he said. "You've got it."

Wendy seemed okay. But Mark, no use in alarming Robert, looked to be in emotional trouble. After she got up to put on another record, Marina went into her workroom and fetched her portfolio of drawings and renderings. "My children," she said. It was clear he didn't know what to make of them, but she made him look anyway. She watched him looking at them and saw parts of him march past—the sneer of a Richard Nixon, the lopsided hair and gaunt openness of a John Kennedy, the self-conscious folksiness of Garrison Keillor, the self-absorption of a Gary Cooper cowboy. She knew he was thinking the phrase, "Who are you?" He was wondering, "Who is this tall, strong woman whose house I seem to have eaten dinner in?"

"Have you ever gone up in a two-seater plane?" he asked.

"No."

"Would you like to go? I could take you. We could go on a picnic."

"We could."

She knew what his wife felt. She knew what it was like to sit on the deck in Newport, to think, "This was our house and now I'm here alone in it." She saw as Pam did that there were as many good reasons for Robert not to leave as there were to leave.

Marina's sense of experience raced ahead of her; she knew about going up in a plane with him as if she'd already done it. She'd dress simply, try to make it as ordinary an excursion as possible. But the excitement, the wind pulling at her jacket and tossing her hair would make a fashion of the simplicity.

At first the plane would feel and sound like a willful old car without a muffler. He would laugh at the sound of it and she would laugh, too. Then there would be some pilot-performance—a show of looking at the panel and pulling at the throttle and guiding the small aircraft—a message of, "This is what I know how to do."

And then, for a while, it would be like a roller coaster. She would think, "Why did I want to do this? Take me down." She would say something like, "I'm not sure I'm going to like this."

He would say, "If you get frightened, just say the word and I'll take you down."

But before she knew it, they'd have gotten up high to where the landscape below became clear and beautiful while at the same time, the ride smoothed out. They would sit back, they would actually talk.

He'd ask, "What do you think?"

She'd say, "I think I'm fine. I think I like it."

"Good, good," he'd say. "If this baby were bigger, we could fly the whole way to Colorado," he'd joke.

"Find Hedy, feed her, and take a run over the land."

He'd look at her. His pupils would fill up his whole eyes (as they often did anyway). It would look like the sky was coming right through his head. She would look away, seeing the towns and suburbs below as he named them.

Without looking back she would be able to picture exactly the line of his body, the wrinkle of his clothes, the direction and fall of his hair, not particularly long but uneven as a well-used brush. She would recognize that she had not escaped the fate of being stupidly, entirely in love.

At one point she would look at him and she would catch a split-second glimpse of his depression, his boredom with the airplane, and his fatigue at being at the controls. When he knew she saw, he'd smile and behave as if some pesky decision or bit of timing had been at stake moments before. Still, in spite of the lie, her feeling would not be shaken, and this would be very confusing and odd. She would study the view and eventually see in the distance a tiny speck, then a larger and larger dot on the landscape, then a person. All the while she would take comfort from the thought, "That person is like me." The speck, become a person, would wave them down with long, slow, confident sweeps of the arms. The patience and confidence of the movements would be mesmerizing.

They would linger for a moment and then obey the waving figure, beginning the landing—not acceptable, but what choice did you have?

WEEDS

When Claire answered the phone and heard Sam's voice, her hand began to shake. He'd always called her during the day, never at dinnertime like this when her husband was home.

He said, "Meet me down by the Giant Eagle. At the back where they load in. I don't know the name of the street."

She said, "Sorry, no, I don't plan to contribute." She thought she should hang up, but she couldn't. Her legs trembled, too. She wasn't eager to get back to the table.

He laughed. "Why is it I don't believe you?"

"We bought tickets last year," she said, stretching to the sink to pick up a cloth she used to wipe splashes from the stove.

"Just do it. Seven o'clock."

She didn't pick up the cloth. "I'm sorry. We can't buy again this year." In the silence she could hear the kitchen clock over the stove whirring. She turned to look at it.

"Eight o'clock."

"No."

"Nine. My last offer. Just get there." He hung up.

For a few moments, Claire stood near the sink, listening to a dial tone. She could just see through the frame of the kitchen door into the dining room; she could just see Franklin's coarsely curly hair and the back of his oxford-cloth blue shirt.

Without pretending to speak to anyone further, she replaced the receiver. Her eye caught the butter, which she'd forgotten to put on the table. By the time she got a knife for it and cleaned up its rough edges, she was able to re-enter the dining room.

Franklin was slicing another piece of roast beef. "What was that all about?" he asked as he put the roast beef on his plate. "The phone call?" he added when she didn't answer.

"Oh, the police benefit. Circus tickets for underprivileged children."

"I thought that was in October."

"There seems to be another one." Claire buttered a roll, which she didn't really want. "Half?" she offered.

"God, no, I couldn't. You shouldn't let them get into their spiel. Just hang up right away. We ought to get Caller ID. We're getting it at the office. But until then, we just have to be tough."

"You're right." Her heart thumped and she found herself, underneath the chitchat, trying to figure out a way to get out of the house at nine. And this was her life with him these last months, her conversation, oh, so ordinary, her mind, her body, somewhere else entirely. She ate the half roll she'd begun, and looked at the other half on her plate. "Oh, what the hell. . . ," she said as she reached for it.

Franklin reached over and rubbed her hand with the heel of his hand before she raised the roll to her mouth.

At five minutes to nine Claire drove up the slanted loading dock of the Giant Eagle. Her heart pounded almost unbearably as it had for more than two hours now.

The butter she fetched from the kitchen and the extra roll she forced herself to eat had provided her an excuse to leave the house. At eight-thirty she had donned her sweats and told Franklin she needed to burn off a few calories at the gym.

"This time of night?"

"They're open till ten. Maybe later on weekdays."

"That's what *I* should do," he said, but he hauled the pile of papers he had just taken out of his briefcase to the dining-room table, the working end, opposite where they ate. He sat down and held his head up with his hands. "Damned city councillors. All they know is give you more forms to fill out."

"I'm sorry," Claire said. She saw that it was twenty minutes to nine, too early to start out.

"Not your fault." He uncapped his pen and began to write neatly on the xeroxed copies of the forms his secretary would type out tomorrow.

Claire went into the kitchen and wiped off the stove while she watched the Cable News Network. All the while she kept thinking Franklin was going to ask why she didn't just go if she was determined to exercise at night. If he asked, maybe she would change her mind. But he didn't say a word, nothing at all. She took a long look at him before she went. But no matter how she talked to herself or what good things she saw in him, she couldn't imagine not going.

Sam's car pulled up, near hers, just on the other side of the banking wall. An old tank of a car, the engine loud and scratchy. Claire began to open her door; she was planning to get into Sam's ancient Chevy. She usually did just that, hopped into his car, and he drove off, to somewhere. She'd made love to him often enough on the backseat of his car, and somehow in the rush and grapple of their lovemaking, the faded rose vinyl, the smell of gasoline, and the grit and dirt of the car helped her forget everything at home, allowed her to forget who she was.

But Sam was getting out of his car, too. He motioned to her to close her door and she did. He came around to her passenger door and knocked. When she saw him through the window, she saw him as if for the first time. He still wore the jeans and sweatshirt with the sleeves cut off, which he must have worn all day working in one yard after another. He looked as if he'd emerged from a dark tunnel somewhere, another world.

"Your car tonight," he said, when she opened the door. "You can't park here. This is the loading dock."

"Right." She had the familiar sensation of wanting to do without words when Sam was around. They seemed silly, bland, and useless.

"Anyway," he said, stretching out. "I wanted to be in your car tonight."

Backing out of the driveway, Claire wondered why. Her car was newer, smaller, more cramped. She was suddenly uncomfortable, embarrassed, too, a grown woman sneaking off to make love in the backseat of a *respectable* car. This wasn't the same at all, this going in her car. He must be planning to take her someplace.

"I don't know where to go," she said, her hands open and light on the steering wheel.

"Down the boulevard, over the bridge. I'll tell you when to turn right."

As Claire turned out of the parking lot, two of her neighbors, teenage boys, waved to her. One held a bag of groceries, the other tagged along. She pretended she didn't see them, but when she slowed down before merging into the regular street traffic, one of them did a rat-a-tat on her trunk. She waved without turning around to see which boy it was. One of them lived next door. Would he tell his family about Sam in the car? Would he think it was nothing? Kids had no idea what adults did. And whatever kids did was, in spite of what they thought, so innocent. These boys played football in the street outside her house for hours and hours of an evening, most days. That's where their minds were, she persuaded herself.

All along the street that led to the boulevard, people walked hand in hand. "How odd. I've never noticed so many hand holders before," she said.

"Maybe it's a law around here." He made it sound suggestive. He made everything sound that way.

"Maybe." She looked over at him, trying to match his tone.

Only blocks from her home, Claire had a fear, unreasonable surely, that she would see Franklin, that he would have left the house and been driving around the neighborhood. When she got further on, to the bridge, the warehouses, and fast-food restaurants, she sighed deeply, felt finally more anonymous.

The first time Claire saw Sam she was dressed up in a good sweater and skirt, heels, earrings, the whole bit. Ever since, she has almost always dressed up to climb into the back seat of his car, to go to a deserted road someplace or the woods, to be stripped. She has the feeling that Sam likes to see her dressed up, even remote and unapproachable-looking, somebody that people might think unsensual. She thinks she looks unsensual most of the time. It's just a look that she was born with, a New England good-schools-and-all sensible look. Wide forehead, medium coloring. She wears her longish brown hair blunt cut, clean and classic.

"I can see you," Sam said, at the beginning. "I know what's going on in there. I think you're just going to have to meet me out on the road someplace. 'Bout time something good happened to you."

At first she hated him for coming so close to her. Now she often fantasized about leaving Franklin, going off with Sam. Every day, morning and night, she would let Sam take possession of her until the hunger ended. Where would they be? A small apartment someplace. A motel. He told her he lived in a 'hole in the wall' somewhere in Coopersdale. She imagined that she would change things, slowly, get him to wear something other than work clothes. She would make dinners. He would become transformed into a man with a history and a future, a man with ideas. She could walk down the street with him, holding hands, and it wouldn't be odd. She knew that none of this made any sense, but thoughts came up like weeds, unbidden, the worse they were, the stronger. The more persistent and damaging.

Before she got to the bridge Sam said, "In about a half mile, you turn right." He reached over and touched the waistband of her sweatshirt. "Different," he said. "Not your usual thing." He let his hand fall against her and let it move with the motion of the car.

By the time she drove into the grounds of the reform school where Sam directed her, even though she laughed at the idea of it, where they ended up, she felt half crazy with wanting him. Ahead of them was a huge gate, but it appeared to be untended by anything other than an electronic eye. She might have been anywhere. All around them at the entry way, leaves shimmered in the moonlight.

"I spent some time here a couple of years ago," Sam laughed. "Yep. I know these woods pretty well." He pointed to a path and then another. Claire drove slowly with the lights off. The second path seemed only wide enough for two people walking, but when Sam nodded, she drove into it.

Claire shut off the engine and looked around her. She was only two miles from home. "What were you in reform school for?" she asked.

"To learn a trade?" he laughed. "To take up gardening?"

"No, really?"

"No, really...."

Claire couldn't tell if others thought him handsome, as she did. He paid no attention to how he looked, probably told an old barber somewhere every six months or so to trim his hair, to leave it a little longer in back than in front. And yet, he looked wonderful.

Claire reached toward him, combed her fingers though his dark brown hair, felt again its thick texture, its natural oils, its richness. When he kissed her, she closed her eyes and tasted the now familiar hints of cigarettes, beer, onions. None of the smells was unpleasant, mixed as they seemed to be, with the fortune of good health. And he smelled of sweat, too, and of leaves and of dirt.

"I thought about you all day," he said. "All day. Almost every minute."

Claire shifted in his arms, let him move her around. She thought that this could go on forever, just this way, her own crazy arrangement. Another part of her knew that this had to end soon.

In the back seat, which they reached by climbing over the front seat—the car doors might have made too much noise —Sam had her clothes off in a minute. He slid himself into her, saying, "Isn't this good?"

"It's good," she breathed. She thought, "I love you," but she didn't say it.

Sam said, "Tomorrow morning at nine o'clock. Again. Right here."

"I can't," she said.

"Oh, yes you can. Tomorrow morning you drive right here to this spot. I'll fuck you real good tomorrow morning. Right here." He stopped moving for a moment, looked at her and laughed.

"I don't think there's any way," she said. In a flash she thought about her job interview at ten, an important job interview, too, but she put it out of her mind. She couldn't talk to him about things like that. Or didn't.

"And at three tomorrow afternoon. We'll meet here, but maybe we'll go someplace different. Find someplace new."

Later she twisted out of his embrace and asked, "You were joking, weren't you?"

He threw back his head and laughed. "Not a joke. Nine o'clock and three o'clock. And you don't get home for supper tomorrow night. Not until late, anyway. Not until old Franklin has to find something on his own."

"Don't talk about him like that."

"Don't? Okay. We'll just think it."

Claire managed to pull away from him. "He's never done anything to you," she said.

"I know. I just like to imagine he has."

For a moment Sam looked dreamy. He gazed out of the back window of the car, comfortable, it seemed. What did he look at? The trees? The moon? Where would he take her tomorrow? Finally, a place. Maybe his apartment. After all, what else was possible? Someone might see them if they went to the Ramada or the Holiday Inn. An old movie came to mind, *A Touch of Class*. Maybe she could put fresh flowers on the table of the kitchen of the small, awful apartment.

"Nothing bad will ever happen to you," Sam laughed. It hurt her bones when he moved. "You look like somebody's grade school teacher."

She'd wanted once to be a grade school teacher. Might have been a grade school teacher if she'd taken a few other turns. But she ended up neglecting the education courses and getting a master's in history, which landed her in the historical society for a while, until funds ran out. She was now out of work and hoping for the job with the county's Senior Citizens Program she would apply for the next day.

"Nine o'clock and three o'clock."

Claire didn't protest because she had made a small agreement with herself never to say no to Sam.

Claire drove into the grounds of the Atkins Detention Center at eight fifty-five the next morning. In the brightness of the morning, she couldn't ignore the gate or the guard who motioned her to stop. "Where are you going?" he asked.

To pull up to the guard, she'd had to pass the entrance to the path she drove down last night. "I'm going to visit my nephew," she said.

"Not until three. Three till five."

"My sister asked me to check on him. They're making an exception."

The guard waved her through. She watched him through the rearview window, watched him watching her. It would be impossible to turn back out of the gate and down the footpaths with the guard keeping track of her. She made a guess and kept going straight. She parked the car at the edge of a parking lot. A building was a few hundred feet away, but the woods were to her right. She got out of the car and walked to the edge of the woods. From where she stood, the guard was not in sight.

She was wearing heels, but the path was dry enough that she could walk carefully. She would walk for five or ten minutes, trying to find the place where she met Sam last night. If he got into the grounds, and he probably would somehow, he would know she'd done this for him. She looked at her watch. She'd gotten her interview moved to ten-thirty.

Surprisingly, she found the spot before she'd walked three minutes. As she turned in a circle, she realized it wasn't that far in the woods. Through the trees she could just see the building of the detention center. If she walked another hundred feet in the other direction, she imagined she would be able to see the guard.

There was no place to sit down, so she leaned against a tree. After a while she took off her shoes and planted her feet on a clear, bare patch of ground. No use kidding herself. It didn't matter that she imagined an apartment and a transformed Sam, someone who lived in the world. He would never be that, and yet he was perfect the way he was. He was her means of understanding that she had to leave Franklin. She knew that. She'd always known it.

She might never mention Sam to her husband. The fact of Sam would hurt Franklin more than he deserved to be hurt. She would get herself a job, get herself an apartment, leave

Franklin, and then deal with Sam. Who was showing a new characteristic. He was late. Very late.

At ten o'clock she started back through the woods.

She said to the guard on the way out, "Thanks, he's doing well." Although she kept moving and didn't look back, she imagined the guard waving her out.

When Claire arrived home at twelve she stood in the kitchen and looked at the phone as if it might answer her questions by ringing. After a while she made herself a roast beef sandwich and stood at the counter eating it. She kicked off her shoes, drank a glass of iced tea, and went upstairs to change clothes. She left her things on the bed and put on jeans, a sweatshirt, and her most comfortable shoes, old Docksiders, and sat on the edge of the bed. On the nightstand on Franklin's side was the book he was reading and an address book. She stretched back and picked both up.

The novel was called *Country Season*. On the back cover were snatches of good reviews preceding one paragraph of summary. A character named Harry Evereston gave up his job in a stock brokerage firm and bought a house in the country. He became poor in every way, lost not only his money, but his connections, his family, and finally his self-respect. However, the paragraph suggested that something good happened to him at the end, that something came of it all.

Did Franklin feel that way? That he'd like to chuck it all and go to the country? As the tax accountant for all city government offices, he was drowning in paperwork. If he did want to chuck it all and go to the country, she could understand that. Without editing the thought, she realized that she imagined going with him.

He got this job ten years ago, just before she met him. He'd been handsome and hopeful then, a man-about-town of twenty-five. She was twenty-two then. They felt so lucky, they thought people looked at them wherever they went.

Now she felt old before her time. She'd put off having a child, saying that thirty-five was her age limit. Even though she still had three years to go, she felt it wasn't going to happen. Two years ago when the funds at the historical society had run out, it hadn't been all that easy to find another job. And she'd gotten huffy about it and probably lost a few just by being in the wrong frame of mind. There was a good chance that today's interview had reversed things. The committee had been encouraging. The truth of the matter is she likes old people, always has, even though she doesn't want to be one. She thought all this, still sitting at the edge of the bed.

In her lap was Franklin's address book, which she'd picked up when she picked up the novel he was reading. She opened it and looked at his handwriting. She didn't read the addresses, just the shape and stress of her husband's handwriting. Running her finger over the pages, she thought perhaps she could find him.

Once she had begun this ritual, she gave into it completely. At the bureau, she opened one drawer after another and looked at her husband's clothes. Shorts and tee shirts were neatly folded. Her work. Casual shirts, knit shirts. The faded red, the yellow, the faded blue. Why did he like the blue best? She did, too. Why? The material was softer to the touch, that was it.

At the closet she took out one of his sportscoats, then a sweater on a hanger. She brought them to her face. They smelled like him, soapy, human, a faint trace of deodorant. In the bathroom, she ran her hands over his toothbrush, still wet, and his razor, thinking about him. He had been an active child. His parents had loved him, but his father was too strict; he was overweight as a teenager, turned handsome and trim in college, a new man. Still, even then, he'd had a slightly hurt look about him, as if the punishments inflicted by his father would not quite recede to the past. Now he is starting to put on weight again. Maybe it's some cycle repeating.

Sam does not call.

This affair with him has been going on for almost a year. The first few times they made love were months apart. Each time Claire thought of what she did as a singular, bizarre event with no explanation, not to be repeated, never to be talked about. In the last few months, Sam summoned her more and more often. Instead of blocking out what she had done, instead of trying to forget it, Claire found herself working the affair into her life, letting her life rupture.

When at two o'clock he has not called, Claire decides that she will not try to meet him today. She will wait for an explanation before she decides what to do.

At two forty-five, in spite of what she has resolved, Claire gets into her car and drives to the grounds of the detention center. The same guard is at the gate. He doesn't smile. "What's it all about, lady?" he asks. "You didn't visit any nephew this morning. We keep records of all that."

Claire is about to say, "I'm taking a drawing class. I wanted to sketch the trees," but she says instead, "I lied. I was planning to meet someone here."

"Not here you don't," the man says. His arms hang stiffly at his sides, a hint that he wishes he could swing them, maybe hit something. "I'm not going to lose my job over you," he sputters. "Get out. Go on."

But a moment later, as she puts the car into reverse, she hears him say, "Wait a minute. Just a minute. Who were you meeting here?"

Claire looks at him, she hopes, incredulously, and drives off.

Just as she nears the corner of the Giant Eagle, she sees Sam's car. Her heart races. Was she supposed to meet him here? The Chevy is in a different spot than where he'd parked it last night, near the loading lock. She parks two lanes away and waits.

After a few minutes he emerges from the store. For a moment, in the same instant, she both recognizes him and doesn't recognize him. He wears clean clothes, not fashion clothes, but nice cotton pants and a sweater. In his arms is a full bag of groceries.

Claire manages to get out of her car and to reach his car just as he does. "Where've you been?" she asks quietly.

For a split second he looks confused, then almost frightened. "Jesus. You didn't really go, did you? In broad daylight? I . . . I never thought you'd do that." He whistles through his teeth. He looks ugly, the muscles of his mouth in a snarling position, like a dog's or a horse's.

At home, Claire lies down on the bed she shares with Franklin. She is finally crying. She has been wanting to do this for a long time. In high school, she and her friends, used to call a good cry, "having a bath." She is having one hell of a bath. Where will she go, what will she do when she has left Franklin?

Eventually Franklin gets home. She hears tentative exploratory noises downstairs as Franklin looks for her. Because she's crying, she doesn't call out to him. Outside, neighborhood boys whistle or call to each other in hoarse, strange voices. Then after what seems a long time, she hears Franklin climbing up the stairs, each step intensifying her dread.

He sits beside her on the bed. "What is it? Honey? The interview?"

She can hardly remember the interview. She manages to tell him that she might even have gotten the job, that she'll know in a few days.

"Well, what is it?" Franklin tugs at his tie and struggles to get his shirt button open. He looks large and frightened. "Are you sick?"

"I haven't been happy," she begins. "Not sick, but a kind of sickness. Unhappiness is a kind of sickness. I've got to make some changes."

He just looks at her, worried.

"I've got to leave you."

"Jesus," he says. He stands and then sits down again. "What's happened? Something's happened today. What is it? You've got to talk to me."

"It's not something that happened today." Even as she says this, she isn't sure if it is true or not. She feels the ridiculousness of trying to tell him anything serious while he sits at the edge of the bed and she lies there. She sits up and looks straight at him. He moves so that she can adjust her legs. With no where else to put them, she gets into a yoga position. She is afraid he won't take her seriously, so she keeps meeting his eyes, realizing at once that she has not met his eyes, like this, for a long time. "I'm sorry," she persists. "There's no good time to say something like this. And there's so little to say. I'll be the one to leave."

"Are you serious?"

"Yes."

"But you haven't even told me what's wrong." He does not look surprised, only confused and needing all the facts. He looks as if he expects difficult things, as he does when he works at a huge pile of papers, determined. He reaches past her and switches on a lamp.

She stands up. It seems to have become evening suddenly. Not dark yet but moving toward it.

The phone rings. She knows as fully as she's ever known anything that it will be Sam. She feels it all coming to a close. In the pause in which Franklin looks distractedly at the phone, Claire takes the few steps to the phone and answers it.

"Hey, look," is all she hears. She hangs up.

"I can't exactly say there's someone else," she says. "I've been having sex with someone else. Sneaking off. I couldn't tell you why. I don't know myself. I don't know. I really don't know."

"Last night?"

She answers him slowly. "Yes, last night. You mean you knew?"

"No, I thought it and put it out of my mind as impossible. Not impossible but unlikely." Franklin stands, his tie still in his hand. "Do you love him? Are you running off with him?"

Claire shakes her head and laughs as she tells him, "No. Not that he'd want me to." But the sound she makes is harsh and tense.

In the small space at the foot of the bed, Franklin paces. She fancies she sees him for a moment, in an office, at a meeting. "I'm trying to understand. You love him, but he doesn't love you? Is that what you're saying?"

Outside the evening routine begins—more shouts and the occasional sound of a football hitting the street pavement. The area outside their house has an especially wide expanse of street without parked cars, heaven to boys.

This is not at all how Claire expected it to be. She expected Franklin to say something angry and leave the house. Storm out of the house. She imagined she would pack a few things and leave while he was gone. He would have the dignity of his fury. She would have the dignity of her aloneness. But, of course, he wants answers. And she hardly has them to give him. The history of this breakup won't come clear to her.

"Love probably doesn't have anything to do with it," she says. "It's not that kind of thing."

"What kind of thing was it then?"

Was? "He's not particularly nice to me. I know, that's an insult to you. It's just fucking, that's all. In the backseat of his car, usually. An old car. And he doesn't even change clothes for our dates. He's still in dirty jeans and tee shirts with the smell of garden chemicals and peat on him. All right? Do you know enough? That's what I've become."

She gets up and stands at the window, waiting for him to say something. For a long time, he doesn't. While she waits, she turns slightly and her eye falls on his address book and the novel he is reading.

"He's a gardener? How did you meet him?"

"He was working next door. I offered him a glass of water."

"You started it then. Maybe you love the guy, even though you won't say it. Maybe you think he should be more something or other to justify all that's been going on. I don't know. But if it's been going on, if you started it, then it's something. I take it seriously, even if you don't. Look. I need some time to breathe. I'm going to go downstairs. Fix myself a drink. I don't want to lose you, if you're asking. But I think I already have. I don't think I can deal with that right now."

Claire hears him going down the steps, heavily. She looks out the window at the approaching evening. The boys will play on the street until it gets completely dark. At the corner of the neighbor's yard is the very spot she first saw Sam, happy, working in the garden, whistling and moving fast. He glistened from sweat, his face was wet with the efforts of his exertion. He seemed to have no need for anybody, he looked so self-sufficient to Claire a year ago. She took him a tall glass of water with ice in it. For some reason, even at the time, she thought of him as somebody biblical, someone who had come on a long journey. She was just the local beautiful woman at the well, giving what she could in the way of sustenance.

You never could guess about people. You never knew how crazy they were or their backgrounds. How was she to know the man in the yard needed to disrupt her life? How could she know that she was crazy enough to jump in? She thinks now about her two visits to the detention center today. They seem to have been made by another person. Who could have seen it in her?

Her lover had been in reform school. For what? Stealing cars, fighting, drugs? He is only twenty-five. Ten years ago he did something bad enough to warrant being sent away from his family. She sees him clearly, a boy who hasn't grown into adulthood, what some people call a loser.

Outside the boys call to each other. One boy trips another and laughs. The other rights himself slowly, working, as he picks up the ball, to fight back from defeat. The boys play forever, even when the streetlights come on and the street is gray with dusk. She can't imagine why they don't go home or how they can see at all what they're doing.

SMALL ERRANDS

Just about every day from late May until early October, in spite of the steadily increasing and almost overwhelming tourist crowds, Linda went out for milk or bread, to mail a letter or to check the sales on paper products at the discount store. Something. And every day when she went out, she drove around Washington Street or up Jefferson Street where she could see Washington Street. Mostly she passed the post office, but sometimes she scanned the cars in the Acme lot, sometimes even the small lot by the hardware store. Usually she had the baby with her. "It's all right, Peter darling," she would say. "We're just driving around. We're just looking at who's here." When she took Peter out of the car to go into a store, she tried not to hold him too tightly, although she often wondered if he felt the tension anyway. She'd catch herself murmuring into his ear, nuzzling his neck all the while, murmuring over and over, "It's all right. We're all right. We're okay."

The whole time, from May to October, Linda felt as if she were walking in a dream. Peter woke up several times a night. So, she was tired, that was one thing. And some of her pregnancy weight was still on her, a cushion between her old self and the world. "Hey, little honey," she'd say. "I hope you love your fat old Mama. I hope you love your fat old crazy Mama."

She was looking for, but not really expecting to find, a bronze station wagon, make unknown, but she thought it was a Dodge from another she'd seen that looked a lot like it. The one she wanted would have a license plate with a P and a Q in it somewhere and on the back window ledge a box of some off-brand of wet-wipes. Some other detail lodged in her brain, but she couldn't locate it. Yet she thought she would know the car if she saw it. The car had been driven by a woman who had tried to steal her child.

The woman had disappeared. Nobody knew anything about her, not even if she'd ever done such a thing before. The police asked all the usual questions: What did the woman look like? Can you remember the rest of the license plate? Can you recall anything else about the car?

No, she answered to most of their questions. She had told them everything she knew: The woman was small in a shrunken way, probably not very old but with a very creased face, wearing an ordinary skirt of some sort and a muted plaid short-sleeve shirt, had short dark hair, somewhere between brown and black, probably dyed. The street and the post office had been relatively empty that day, a surprisingly cold May day, but the few people who were questioned simply couldn't remember any better than Linda what the woman looked like. They had hardly known she was there. An elfin woman dressed out of a 1950s movie, that was about it. Great.

By the end of September and the beginning of October, Linda wished she could forget the woman and tried to will herself not to look for the car.

"What do you think about when you go so still?" Michael asked quietly one evening at dinner. "You're far away, you know. Been that way for a long time now." His muscular body was tight, his eyes bright with restless, unexpressed anger.

She didn't tell him she looked for the woman each day, that she knew she wasn't her old self anymore. She wanted their old life back, but she knew she had lost face with him. He was Greek. She was not. Any Greek woman, he said, would have killed the would-be kidnapper. Linda had no taste for tragedy. She was not reckless but, if anything, a little too polite. If the ability to function could be stolen away from a person, the woman had ruined her. The woman didn't get Linda's baby, but she got her comfort, her faith.

"I think it's the extra weight I'm carrying," she said to Michael. "I hate it. It makes me feel old." But she wasn't really worried about getting her looks back. She was trying to keep a conversation with Michael going, replacing big truths with tiny ones.

"You'll get back to yourself," Michael said. Then he widened his eyes and said, "I hope."

An unacceptable joke and she let him know it with a glance. He hadn't really looked at her, wanted her, for a long time. They were in trouble, and yet they went on and on and on. No affection in his eyes, and he had a new tautness in his body, a defiant message of self-sufficiency. She didn't call him on it! She was afraid if she screamed now she'd lose him completely.

"Let's go out, movies, jazz, whatever, when my mother comes," she suggested. "Like the old days. Mom says that's her gift to us."

"Keep pushing me to get ahead on the article so I can clear a couple of nights."

"I'll push." She didn't really want to urge him to work more. He already spent most of his time at the college and when he was home in his den at the computer, staring at the screen, changing things.

For the adult portion of her nearly thirty years, Linda had seemed like the kind of person who in any emergency would perform like a Florence Nightingale. She'd thought of herself that way, too. People trusted her. In her job as loan officer at the bank, she'd said yes as often as she could, but she also knew how to deal with angry people licking the wounds of insult if she had to let them down. She was practical. She caught when she was being short-changed, could organize a party or meeting in minutes, saw when a friend was troubled and knew how to draw that friend out. Nobody thought she was crazy. But maybe she was. She was living a sham marriage with Michael. And she had crazy thoughts. Sometimes she thought of going for a walk with the baby and leaving the stroller somewhere unattended. A way of playing chicken with the woman in the bronze car. Packing a bag and leaving everyone.

In late September Linda got a letter from her mother and handed it toward Michael as he was settling in to watch the evening news. "My mother's coming in *five days*," she said. "Remember?"

"I'm certainly not ahead. Maybe behind."

She knew the article was driving him crazy. It was about the economies of Greece and Turkey. "We don't have to...."

"It's okay," he said, waving her silent.

They watched the news. Linda poised at the door to hear Peter's tiniest cry, the letter still in her hand. There was a traffic accident on one of the highways, a terrible thing, with a truck hitting several cars stopped in the emergency lane. A woman had used her body to protect her baby. The woman died, but her baby lived. She and Michael watched with an intensity that made a quiver go through her stomach. A lovely woman, young, joyful. Linda looked at the woman's photograph and cried.

She hadn't been prepared for disaster. Whoever is? She had gone to the post office pushing Peter in a stroller. She remembered the events in simple broad gestures—how she had moved the stroller to a spot next to the counter, how she had moved forward a foot or so to make her order for stamps and to collect a baby present that had arrived by mail with postage due, how she had turned back to the stroller moments later to see it empty, her son gone.

She had dropped the package and run out of the post office toward a woman who was carrying Peter over her shoulder like a practiced nursemaid. Linda tried to yell, "Stop," but her voice disappeared on her. She was astounded, fascinated by the woman's seeming sureness.

She caught up to the woman. She pulled at Peter, saying, "Give me my baby back. Give me my baby," in a voice she didn't even recognize.

The woman looked at her and said simply, "Stop that. He's my baby. This is my baby," in a calm voice that suggested Linda was the crazy one.

Linda pulled at Peter again, as hard as she could. The woman held him so tightly Linda thought she might hurt him if she pulled again.

Then in a sudden move, the woman turned and started walking fast toward the street.

It was insanity, the whole thing, impossible to describe even though she kept trying later. Linda screamed, a small sound at first, then louder as the woman kept walking. The horror of it paralyzed her. She collapsed. All she could do was scream. Linda later read in the newspaper that she had "screamed like Greek tragedy," which was an odd, possibly intentional, joke on the part of the journalist. People said the sounds that came out of her were awful. She didn't remember. All she knows is she failed to act, to move. Maybe there was some sort of hypnosis involved. Or, there must have been a part of her that wanted to be done with something, finished. Shock, people said. Her friend Bonnie had told her she was in deep shock, the screams were a primitive system of fighting, and they had worked.

At the sound of the screams, the kidnapper had put Peter down on the sidewalk, not carefully, more like a thief dropping a bag of stolen groceries. Then the woman went to her car and suddenly, carelessly, backed up close to the sidewalk, and just as suddenly drove away.

That was when people came running. Linda rose and went to her baby, lifted him, took off his blanket and examined him for injuries, thinking the whole time how lucky it was that newborns were soft and not easily hurt. Still, she told people who gathered around to get the police and an ambulance. She dispatched someone to call Michael. She wrapped Peter up again and held him. Then Peter began to cry. Nothing Linda did could calm him that day.

Shock, the doctors explained, patting him. Babies experience shock, too, they said. But he was a healthy little bugger. He'd be fine.

Now as she watched Michael turning off the news, she asked, "Do you still think about it?"

"I try not to," he said. He got up and stretched.

"I think I think about it every minute."

"Try to forget it. We were lucky."

"But you blame me still." She could see that he was already starting to say no. "I'd rather talk about it."

"No," he said. "I don't blame you. Honestly." He held her in a way he hadn't for a long time. The touch was deep and comforting.

She almost asked him why nobody was able to find him that day, but she couldn't bear to break the embrace. Maybe they weren't ready for that conversation. Not yet. Or she wasn't.

That night Linda stood behind Michael as he worked at the computer in his den, once more oblivious to her. She wished certain things in life could be wiped out by pointing the cursor at them and putting something else in their place. It seemed a wonderful thing, the select and delete function.

How long do people go on this way, she wondered. Years, she's heard.

"Oh, sweetheart," Linda's mother said, standing inside the front door. "My little darling." Her mother was a plump blonde woman who had cultivated a dimpled look. She was cute, in her pretty rose-colored blouses and her little bits of jewelry. Today she wore earrings Peter would certainly want to pull and plopped down a suitcase full of her other clothes. "You just take care of yourself, honey," she told Linda. "Your good old Mama's here, your good old loving Mama's right here to take care of things."

It was supposed to be a treat, a comfort, having someone trusted and competent take over. But after two days, Linda felt ragged and at odds. How many leisurely baths could she take after all? At her mother's suggestion, she got a new haircut, a sleek wedge, and her honey-colored hair picked up a shine again. Her mother insisted she do her nails right, not just slap a coat of polish over them. How silly. What did these things matter? She told her mother there was too much emphasis put on youth and looks and a carefree attitude. Her mother laughed at her and asked what had spooked her from remembering the essential truths.

On the fourth day of her mother's visit, Michael and Linda were supposed to go out with Bonnie and Jed to hear jazz.

They were supposed to drive up to Wildwood. Linda suddenly had no real desire to go. The weather was gray and damp, for one thing. And Peter was fussy. "Let me hold him," she said to her mother. "I think he's cutting a tooth. It doesn't feel so good, darling does it?" She held him and sweet-talked him, but his bouts of fussiness erupted without any relation to what she did.

"Let me try," her mother said. "Poor little darling. I have a few tricks."

Linda watched her mother make wildly comic faces to distract him. The things people did!

When Michael got home, Linda suggested canceling. "Bonnie and Jed probably wouldn't mind taking a rain check."

Michael practically pushed her toward the bedroom to get dressed. "We need to make the break sometime. Come on, Linda. It's only one evening."

While she put on makeup, Michael lay on the bed and looked at her. She felt a stirring from seeing his eyes examine her and hoped that once again desire was kindling in him, too.

"I get out a little bit every day," she said lightly. "Don't worry about me."

"Well, that's a different thing," he said. "Taking Peter out no matter what the weather. He has a cold now. Your mother said so."

"A tiny cold. Mostly it's his teeth." Linda took off her robe. She was wearing a soft pink full slip, one with lots of lace at the bodice and up the side seams. To think she fit into it again. "All children get colds," she said gently. "When I go back to work again, he'll catch a lot of colds at day care. So I'm told. But he'll learn to fight them off. I'm told."

"I'll be a basket case." He rolled over and continued to look at her.

She was about to tell him it was high time she went back to work, that a whole year at home was too much. Michael sighed as if he guessed what she was about to say. Just then she heard Peter crying and went to wrest him from her mother who was still making bizarre faces at him. "Take a break," she told her mother. She brought Peter into the bedroom and sat on the bed beside her husband.

They were silent for a while. Michael patted his son's leg and lifted him out of his mother's arms.

Sometimes, when she saw Michael relaxed as he was tonight, Linda remembered the first time she ever saw him. He was spending that summer doing work for a contractor who got the renovation job on the bank where she was employed. He had such strong arms, and his skin always looked as if he'd been in the sun. He certainly didn't look like any college professor she'd ever had. He was exotic-looking.

The stress of academic life didn't suit him, and yet it was what he wanted. Linda smoothed her hands over Michael's brow and let them disappear into his worried, thick curly hair. Michael pulled away gently and squeezed his eyes up in a funny squint. When he looked at Linda it was with too blue eyes, as if the color were newly mixed of love and anger.

The din of conversation around them blended with the soaring voices of the instruments. And Linda's voice soared, too, at first just to be heard, later with a genuinely tuned up joy at being out and letting go.

"Looking good," Bonnie yelled. "You're looking good!"

In spite of herself, Linda beamed and shrugged. Things were coming back. The flush of color. Oils in the hair. Hardness in the fingernails. Lightness. She let her friends fuss over her and was amazed at how good it felt.

She'd missed Bonnie and Jed. She'd forgotten how sweet they were, how they were willing to turn somersaults to entertain their friends. When difficult things happened to them, they turned them around and fashioned them into comic routines. They probably practiced at the breakfast table. Linda had a pang of jealousy; the breakfasts at her house were quiet, mute. She and Michael processed things differently, by following the tiniest thread here and there as it reappeared over time, by pressing it out of sight, bringing it back into the picture transformed by silence. There were things she knew just by the order in which he told her. There were things she almost knew about him but didn't want to know.

"So she comes into his office," Bonnie was saying, "moves on up to his desk and says, 'I don't care about grades. I really don't. Go ahead. Flunk me.'" Bonnie tried to say this suggestively and everybody laughed, which seemed to gratify her. She pressed on, imitating. "'Just take me to bed once. I've had the hots for you for three years.'"

"Clearly not a very bright student," Michael said, puckering up his face to force away a smile. Was he laughing at his own joke?

Bonnie hit Michael as twelve-year-old girls hit boys in conversation, playfully but hard. She cast her own husband a flirtatious look and said, "That kid knew what she was doing all right. Instinct or whatever."

"Actually," Jed said proudly, "she is very bright. Really. She came to inquire about her only A minus."

The women hooted at him, trying to tease him about "very bright" and "A minus," but the music swelled to a size that made a witticism impossible to deliver correctly, and the moment passed. Jed looked a little miffed.

"Well, he told me about it, at least," Bonnie said later when the band took a break. "I'm an idiot, you know. In a way I almost admire her guts. Almost! To be that young and that forthright!"

"And that uncomplicated. . . ." Michael mused.

"That full of bravado and desperation," Linda said quietly.

Bonnie poured Linda another beer from the pitcher. "If anyone messed with Michael, you'd probably tear her face off," she said in a tone of congratulation. Linda looked up. It seemed Bonnie stared a message at her, forgetting to look where she was pouring, and foam spilled down the side of the glass and onto the table.

Linda felt blood rush to her face. She shrugged, saying, "I don't know what I'd do." She saw something cross Michael's face, but she wasn't sure what.

Because she was looking at Michael, Bonnie and Jed turned to him, too. He managed to say, with self-mocking charm, "Linda? Somehow I doubt it. She'd say, 'Take him, take him.'"

Everyone laughed. The joke made him seem humble and desirable, his eyes, Aegean blue eyes, dancing between presence and absence.

Through the next round of drinks and jokes, Linda allowed herself to remember. She'd felt Michael disappear just before the almost-kidnapping. She hadn't wanted to know why, but now she knew well enough. Her laughter for the rest of the evening was fake-sounding, harsh.

The next day Linda woke up, determined that she would talk to Michael that night, even if the timing was bad, even if she made a scene when her mother was there. Maybe she could get him to go out again, to someplace local, for a beer. She didn't know what she was going to say. She had no hopes that she would handle it well, but she knew finally that they had to deal with it, the fact that he was off somewhere with someone who was uncomplicated. Or pretending to be. And maybe that was what he wanted.

"Please," her mother said when it was almost noon. They had had several cups of coffee. "Forgive me, honey, but I'm not on a diet. This two-percent milk just makes coffee taste awful to me. It just does. Let me be fat and happy. If you're going out, be a good girl and get your Mama some rich coffee cream."

"I wasn't thinking. Sorry. Hey, I might have a hit of it myself."

It was afternoon when she went out. In the way things happen when you stop thinking about them, she saw the car.

The details she hadn't been able to remember were a decal of a chipmunk on the box of wipes and the oldness of the box. Bronze station wagon, Dodge, PB0923. A sticker from something made the *0* look like a *Q*. Linda didn't write anything down. She thought about what she should do, thought about just going home. Then she parked her car and began to walk.

In a sense she didn't want to find the woman. When the library, the post office, and the few open shops yielded nothing, she stood uncertainly, down the street and a block from the car. She wondered what to do. Ahead she saw a phone booth and headed for it. She would let the police know that she'd seen the car. On impulse, she called her mother first.

"Mother, is everything all right?"

"Super," her mother crooned. "We're all just super. You can take your time. The little fellow loves his grandmother, he does. We're just fine and dandy. Golly, he's going to look like Michael."

"I know. Do me a favor, will you? Don't answer the door until I get home. I know it sounds foolish, but be especially careful. Okay? For my sake, and Peter's sake. Whatever you do, don't let anyone, any strangers, I mean, into the house. All right?"

"What?"

Linda hung up. She had seen something. A small woman, far away, cloth-coated it looked like, going into the delicatessen.

Linda stands in front of one of the three tables in the Darideli, looking at the woman in the gray cloth coat. The woman is drinking a cup of coffee. On the table next to her cup are four opened sugar wrappers. A cigarette burns in the ashtray. The woman looks straight ahead and seems to see nothing. The coat sags and puckers from her being slumped over and turned in on herself.

Behind the meat counter, just next to the rack of potato chips and packaged cookies is a phone. Linda takes one step backwards from the woman and reaches into her pocket for a coin. Finding none, she opens her purse and sees, with relief, both dimes and quarters. When she looks up again, the woman is looking at her.

"Cold day," the woman says. Her voice might be that of any stranger being conversational.

Linda answers, "Yes. It is, has been this year." Her voice sounds shaky to her.

"Get yourself a cup of tea," the woman says. "Warm yourself up."

So. The woman doesn't remember her. Linda finds herself saying, "Yes, good idea." She leaves the pay phone reluctantly and calls out to the man behind the counter to get her a cup of tea. He is an old-timer in Cape May. She wonders if he read the paper last spring, if, like so many other locals, he knows what happened. "With cream and sugar," she adds. She is relieved to hear her own voice. The owner of the deli doesn't seem to recognize her, not even as residents do

each other when they don't have names to go with the faces.
He is mixing up a chicken salad.

"Tea, did you say?"

She says yes, slips into the seat across from the woman
and tries to think how to begin the questioning. Fearing
silence, she simply says, "I'm Linda. And you?"

"My name is Edna," the woman says.

"Edna? Edna what?"

After a pause the woman says sadly, "Barrow." She
fiddles with her restaurant check. Linda can see clearly. It
says eighty-five cents for coffee. Edna lets it fall in the center
of the table.

"Barrow," Linda repeats. "Do you live in Cape May?"

"No, no," the woman almost laughs. "Just visiting for the
afternoon. How about you?"

Linda shakes her head to whatever the question is. "Visiting relatives?" she presses.

"No, no," the woman answers in a little singsong of a
voice. She laughs exactly as she laughed before. "Just visiting the town."

"Did you drive far? I mean, where do you come from?"

Edna Barrow nods and reaches for her coffee. She looks
surprised to see the cup is empty.

"Where do you come from?" Linda repeats. Her own cup
arrives, an unappetizing mug with a tea bag floating on the
surface. "Would you bring this woman another cup of
coffee?" she asks politely, as if she is in the sort of restaurant
that prides itself on service. To Edna Barrow, if that is her
name, she says, "Maybe you'd like something to eat. A sweet
roll?" Edna shrugs indifferently. "Bring two sweet rolls, too."

The woman looks hungry, like a vagrant. Manipulative
and strange, mean and crazy. On the take. On the take, one
way or the other. Linda hates her. Her heart pounds with it.

Maybe minutes go by. Maybe only seconds. It's hard to
tell. "I have a baby," Linda says patiently. "You. . . .took him
out of his stroller once. Last May. Do you remember?"

"No," Edna says. "That wasn't me."

"But it was. Why wouldn't you give him back to me?
Where were you going with him?"

"Children are too much trouble. Who needs it?" Edna smiles unnervingly.

Trying to help! Is that what she means? "No," Linda says, "No. The nature of a child is . . . to be trouble and the nature of a mother is to take this in stride."

"In stride," Edna says.

"Maybe you have children of your own?" Edna shakes her head. She seems far away. Linda can't be sure she's really heard her. "A son? A daughter?" Edna dips her head. Is it a nod? "Did you ever take care of anyone else's children?" There is no answer. "You know. Baby-sit?"

Edna shakes her head no.

Just then the shop owner sets down the coffee and discs of cherry Danish.

"You're very kind," Edna says stiffly. She looks at the roll and coffee. She waits politely, so politely—not touching the Danish—a new drama, a whole new interior script.

"You took my baby out of a stroller in the post office last May," Linda tells her. "I'm the woman who screamed. I screamed like murder. I know you remember. Why did you do it?"

"I don't like you."

"What?"

"I don't like you. You think you can ask me questions."

Linda carefully picks up the checks and leaves them with four dollars under the ashtray. Then she goes to the phone again, half-turning into it for privacy, and calls the police. She wants them to take over. She wants to be done with it all. She tells in a whisper where the woman's car is parked, the license plate, and the name the woman gave her. When asked to give a description, she turns to look at Edna who has begun to eat. She gives details of the coat and the one large bobby pin in Edna's hair. Edna shifts in her seat and watches Linda and continues to eat. She eats her roll and Linda's roll, both. Linda is telling the police, "She seems crazy, out of touch. I've just had coffee with her and tried to talk to her. She's not running or anything."

"Oh?" the police say. "That's odd."

"It is. But you probably should take her in."

Next she calls her mother. "I'm all right," she says. "I know I sounded funny, but I found the woman who tried to take Peter from me. I've got my eye on her. I've called the police. They'll get her, I hope, either here or at her car. Mom? I've got to go."

And then she calls Michael. "No," his secretary says, after doing some checking. "He's gone for the afternoon."

Her breath comes in sharp jabs. Tonight. Definitely tonight. She will not wait until her mother leaves. She doesn't know exactly what she will do. Maybe just scream. Why not start there? She's good at it.

She turns back to the room. Edna is gone.

When Linda gets outside the shop, she lets the breeze touch her for a moment. She lets it bring her the salt air that she loves and that feels as good right now as tears. Her breath hurts. Her chest is full of pain. She hugs her sweater around her and walks to her car. Nowhere, not outside the deli nor down the street on the way to her car, does she see Edna.

There are three policeman standing around Edna's car. From their stance, casual, but guard-like, she concludes that Edna has not yet come back for her car. She gets into her own car, parked some hundred feet away, and thinks she will just coast up to the policemen, identify herself, and reiterate the information she gave on the phone. And yet she finds herself going past them, as if driven by the pounding in her chest, up to Madison Avenue, where she turns around in a driveway and starts back to the deli. She stretches to look inside, then moves through the parking lot to the brightly lighted Acme. If only she could breathe. She thinks, "No, not in there," and drives out of the parking lot. After she checks the bus stop and the parking lot of a restaurant called The Filling Station, she starts on the alleyways behind the mall and then the small backstreets, which lead to the highway, which leads to the end of the island, the point. She opens the car windows, turns on the heater. But she shivers. And still she can't breathe.

As she drives around she forces herself to think of recent conversations with Michael. She dwells upon all the hints of kindness and love. She reinterprets her mother's crooning and hears it all in a fresh way, a nervous longing to help. She pictures Peter as he probably is right now, babbling and crawling around the living room to the applause of his grandmother. She imagines Michael in the best light, in his car, driving fast toward home, giving himself a good talking to about the thinness of uncomplicated women and the value of his not all that thin, not all that crazy wife.

In an alleyway behind the Tomkin's Grill, Linda sees Edna who just stands there, her mouth partway open, her purse dangling from her fingers. Linda sees herself driving right into Edna, imagines Edna's dully surprised look, a purse flying, and somehow, somehow, brings the car to a screeching stop before this happens. She gets out of the car and goes to Edna. Edna whimpers as Linda grabs her wrist and ushers her into the passenger seat. When Linda gets behind the wheel, she stares straight ahead, looking for the police. She can't look anywhere but straight ahead. She must keep going. She knows what she would see if she looked at Edna. A woman frightened, angry, and full of confusion. A face like the furrowed, collapsed face of a newborn.

SIGHTING

To begin with, everything about Ada's life was autumnal. It was November. She was forty-two. She had a strange relationship with a man named Franklin, a relationship which had refused for years to become romantic or sexual and now had its own regular humdrum rhythm. And she was afraid her mother was going to up and die on her.

On weekends Ada rambled around her house, half-heartedly doing the laundry, picking up a pair of shoes left in the living room and putting them into the bedroom closet, nibbling at a slice of cheese, a crust of bread, letting autumn get her down. Her yard was full of leaves and she knew the gutters were, too. This year something had stopped in her—the will or energy to set hands on a ladder or a broom. Or even to call someone to help her take care of things like the yard. How many lists have these maintenance tasks appeared on? How many times has she forgotten to do them?

The truth is she has grown tired of it all—living alone, managing alone—and she toys with the idea of letting her mother move in with her. It may give her that extra push to do things. It may even prolong her mother's wish to live. Of course, it will do some damage, too, to Ada who will immediately fall to servant status. But damage is inevitable, she thinks, as she looks through the dining room windows at the rotting leaves. If she does not do something soon, in spring she will find the gutters crumbling, the spouts clogged, new warps on the picnic table, and rusty blisters like worms on the white yard furniture.

The only thing she has succeeded in doing, apart from getting to work everyday, is planning a trip for her mother, Emma, who lives and works some three miles away from Ada's house. Emma has been sinking into depression and ill health. At the same time, she insists on working fifteen to eighteen hours a day. One of these things is the cause of the other. Ada doesn't know which came first, overwork or a kind of borderline insanity. She guesses that the cure is a change of scene and human contact. So she has rented a cottage in the Pennsylvania woods at Mill Run, and she has somehow convinced her mother and her sister, whose name is Emily, and her sister's family to leave Pittsburgh for the weekend. They will simply sit around and talk and stare at the fire in the cottage. Sleep, eat, and rest.

Emma is a widow who owns an old-fashioned restaurant-hotel combination on the edge of a section of town known as Homestead. She lives in a one-room apartment at the top of the complex in what used to be a small attic. The apartment holds little more than a bed and a spindly cactus which Emma insists is all she needs. She spends nearly all of her time working: cooking, taking cash, serving, even sometimes making the hotel beds. She saves and saves money.

"For what?" Ada asks.

Emma answers that she wants to be able to pay her own way through life with something left over to leave her children and grandchildren. But lately Emma has been operating at a loss. Homestead is blighted by depression, closed steel mills, unemployment. Most of her customers are hotel bums and stragglers who want the daily special, all the spaghetti they can eat for $1.99 or something comparable. Emma's endless soup and salad bar is also popular. Emma talks about selling. Everyone from family to strangers thinks she should. Especially Ada, who would give anything to see her mother get rid of that burden, look at the world around her, rest, live.

As Ada dresses for work on the Friday of the weekend trip, there is a singing at the back of her head, but she doesn't have words for it.

There are few external signs of Ada's decline in spirits. She is perfectly groomed, dressed today, as so often, in white— a woolen skirt and sweater. White is her favorite color. She even drives a white Honda Accord. If she were to turn into an animal, she would be a honey and white cat. She has soft, curly, honey-colored hair, greenish eyes, the spread-out features of a cat's face. Lately, even the lining around the eyes and mouth. Her whole family looks like cats. Beautiful ones, of course.

Self-containedness and purity have always been part of her self-image. As a child Ada used to wish that her middle name were her first name. Diana. Of course, it sounds awful with Ada, as if her mother had stuttered at her birth. But Diana, goddess of chastity, the moon, the hunt, that's who she feels she was named for.

The singing persists at the back of Ada's head as she drives to work. It persists even through the Vivaldi on the tape deck, through her conversation with the parking lot attendant while she searches for money and realizes she does not have enough cash for the cheap lot and will have to go to the expensive lot where she can pay later after she gets to a banking machine. The high note, humming away in her head, persists all through the day.

Ada works for a state agency named Family and Children's Service. She matches parents and children. Sometimes she places children, even up to the age of seventeen, in temporary homes. Sometimes a much-waited-for baby or small child becomes available for adoption. She must choose the couple who wins the prize. There are times she thinks she makes better matches than nature does. This thought occurs to her once or twice the day of the trip.

She tells Nina, a friend from work, that she will skip out early to take her mother out of the city to a cottage in the woods.

"You're a saint," Nina tells her.

"Hardly," Ada laughs. "To tell you the truth, I think it's a guilt trip. You see, if I'm reading the hints correctly, I think my mother wants to come and live with me. To move in."

The idea is enough to stop Nina from eating her potato chips. She is carrying around a Styrofoam plate with lunch on it. "That's serious," she says.

"What's worse is I actually think I may allow it. But I'm no saint. I wouldn't allow it selflessly and purely. I'd be edgy. I want my freedom, just in case I can figure out how to use it."

"Well, Franklin," Nina says. "He might want to move in."

Ada doesn't tell Nina that Franklin just wants to be friends. She can hardly bear to tell herself that. They are very good friends, full of affection and caring. Almost daily phone calls pass between them, and at least once a week they go to a movie or take a shopping trip together. They buy each other Christmas and birthday presents. Everybody assumes it is a sort of lazy romantic relationship. But Franklin just wants to be friends.

"My advice," says Nina, "is don't let your mother move in. And take Franklin to the woods next time."

"Yes," Ada smiles.

At three o'clock she leaves work, stops at home for a small suitcase and the food, which she packs in a Styrofoam cooler. Eggs, cheese, vegetable soup, chicken stuffed with rice and nuts, which her mother requested.

She has been talking to her house lately. She says to it as she leaves, "Fall down if you feel like it. I don't care. I'm leaving you for a cottage in the woods, ha ha. Just don't do anything halfway. If you collapse from lack of attention, I want it total and unfixable." Her bitterness terrifies her. She goes to pick up her mother at the restaurant, "The Homestead." In her mind, as her mother brings a suitcase and a shopping bag to the car, is the picture of her mother packing the cactus and a few other things and moving into Ada's house.

There is still a singing somewhere at the back of Ada's head, but she is busy slicing cucumbers and doesn't pay any attention to it. The neat cucumber slices on the cutting board and the white bowl filled with lettuce are the only things on the counter. The slicing knife causes an almost-echo, the kitchen is so empty. The owners provide only the bare necessities—a threadbare rag rug on the two-tone gray linoleum floor, two knives, three saucepans and one baking tray, chipped blue-flowered china enough to serve six people. And the bowl with the lettuce in it, a lovely pure white fluted china bowl, of much better quality than anything else around.

In the living room on the colonial-style sofa, covered by an afghan of yellow and white squares, is Emma, asleep in front of the fire. This is the reason they have come, so that Emma will rest. Outside the cottage, the trees, almost devoid of leaves but for the last clinging yellow ones, quiver in the wind. It is dark, cold, and wet outside, spare inside but with a habit of yellow touches—the fireplace fire, the flames on the gas stove, the afghan, the lamplight, the roses on the wall paper in Ada's room.

There are three bedrooms here. Ada has one, her mother has another, and the third, which is also the largest, is being saved for Ada's sister, Emily, who will arrive tomorrow with her husband Bob and their child, Melanie. Emma, Emily, Melanie—their names seem to have evolved from each other.

From the refrigerator Ada takes onions and peppers. She cuts them in neat matching sizes as she did the cucumbers. She sings to herself in this bare kitchen, snatches of a country and western song she heard on the radio, and dreams of love. But love is far away, as far as the slice of a moon she can see through the vein-work of branches and twigs that surrounds the cottage.

On the drive here, the hour and a half on the turnpike and the winding roads to Mill Run, Ada's worries about her mother increased. When she took her mother's hand, hugged and kissed her, she felt she was thawing bones. There was a whisperiness to her mother's voice, too. And a heavier than usual sag to the folds of her face. Emma only broke her silence to say that she didn't know where Ada got such a crazy idea as going away for the weekend when they both had perfectly good dwelling places and could get so much accomplished from Friday to Sunday. Ada smiled and said easing things, told funny stories about people at work, made fun of herself and her drifting concentration. She could not bring a laugh, not even a smile, to Emma's face. If Ada could give something to her mother or choose what her mother would give her, it would be laughter. Ada has told her mother many times there are legacies of much greater worth than money, at least to people like them, fashioned of such seriousness.

In the cottage things are calm now. With the established smells of the fire in the living room and the chicken roasting in the oven, it seems hard to believe that Emma tried to cancel out just yesterday, Thursday night, or that she made herself so impossible on the drive here. Emma often rejected things that Ada tried to give her, gifts of sweaters and coats, a refrigerator which Ada had saved up for when she was in college, even a large floor vase, which she had bought with her allowance when she was ten years old. Ada is used to it—so is Emily for that matter—but Ada wishes her mother had the ability to accept love. Ada sprinkles the cucumber slices, peppers and onions over the lettuce. No, she can't quite erase the awareness that her mother would have canceled, given the opportunity. Her feelings are hurt.

With a poke of the fork, Ada determines the chicken is done. She takes it out of the oven and puts it on the table in its baking tray to allow the juices to settle. She tiptoes into the living room and turns on the small stereo radio she brought along. It is sitting on one of two end tables shaped like barrels and placed next to two brown plaid colonial-style chairs that face the matching couch. A coffee table is the only other thing in the room. This cottage is odd, Ada thinks, the owners so reluctant to decorate. Even things one wouldn't choose oneself are interesting, something to touch, something to look at.

After she locates WQED-FM and determines the violin solo they are playing is not too jarring, Ada fades the sound up slowly. She decides that after dinner she will take the flashlight and go for a walk in the woods. Her mother begins to wake.

"Dinner," Ada whispers. "Do you think you can get up?"

"Yes." The answer comes with a trace of accusation. "All right, I'm getting up."

"You said to wake you. I can save the chicken for later if you want."

"I feel like I died." Emma sits up, her hair sticking up in tufts, her eyes still half-closed, a saggy look of sober judgment on her face. "That was a nice fire," she says. The flames crackle as if even the fire has been waiting for a compliment and sputters with joy at having been appreciated.

Some people would be afraid to walk in the woods at night. Ada does not feel afraid. She imagines all around her whole families of animals seeking shelter, burrowing in for the night. Squirrels, raccoons, beavers, deer, all finding their places in the dark. When Ada stops, she can hear the sounds of scurrying, she can hear a trickle of water and a steady vibration of far-away crickets, topped by the cry of an owl. She goes as far as she can until the light from the cottage is out of sight. Then she turns the flashlight toward the sound of water, finds the stream and follows it its long meandering way back to the cottage.

Emma is awake, sitting up in one of the chairs, the afghan over her and tucked behind her. "Where did you go?" she asks.

"Just walking."

Emma peels the afghan off irritably. "I heard all kinds of noises while you were gone. I think a place like this is scary."

"I'm sorry." Ada goes to her and hugs her. "They were probably just 'night in the woods' noises."

Emma nods. "Now I'm ready for pie," she says. She has brought a special-order pie from the restaurant, the kind she gets only at Thanksgiving and Christmas. She arranges the cover around her legs, looking a little like an invalid. She says, "I want to eat it right here. I'm not moving." Her eyes become sleepy again, and she looks straight into the fire, letting it orchestrate the slow drooping of her eyelids and the nodding of her head.

"Are you feeling okay?" Ada asks.

"Oh, don't keep questioning me. I'm just waiting for my pie."

Ada cuts the pie, brings a piece of it on a chipped blue-flowered plate to her mother. "Apple pie," she says. "Here it is." She wonders if the way she cut and served the pie and announced its arrival was an unconscious imitation of her mother at the restaurant. She wishes her mother would stand up, walk, move, laugh, talk. Emma cuts into her piece of pie with her fork and tastes each piece slowly. When the pie is finished, she gets up and trundles off to bed, the afghan now wrapped around her shoulders like a floor-length cape.

At noon on Saturday Emily arrives with Melanie. The door opens on a burst of light as if they brought the sun with them, dissipating fog. Ada likes the noise they make. Melanie carries a bouquet of Queen Anne's lace picked up from the roadside. As she waddles toward her grandmother, she extends it. She is fourteen months old.

Many bags of food have to be carried in from the car because Emily has brought Italian bread and ham, a container of chicken soup, assorted pastries, bagels, salad vegetables, and milk. There are small valises of clothing. A bag of toys for Melanie. The traveling baby bag with diapers and powder and wipes. Emma stands in the kitchen holding the flowers, halted in her attempt to find something vase-like, as Ada helps Emily to load things in. They give Melanie a loaf of bread to carry from the door of the living room to the kitchen, an assignment. She holds it out as she did the flowers to Emma. She is always applauded when she gives, when she helps. This is something Emily feels strongly about. So she puts down her bags and applauds. Melanie is such a willing learner that she grabs the box of graham crackers from the top of the baby bag and hands them to her grandmother.

"Bob had to talk to the contractors again," Emily groans. "At three o'clock no less! He's bringing the van. He'll get here about six. Maybe seven."

When they sit around the table eating the leftover chicken, the talk revolves mostly around the house Bob is building for his family. Ada holds Melanie on her lap and feeds her bits of chicken and stuffing while her mother and her sister talk. Her mother is smiling at Emily who is full of news. "It's good to see you," Emma says. "You look nice."

Melly loves to touch things. When they all go for an afternoon walk, she stoops down to touch the wet leaves on the ground. She runs her hands over the crack in a small tree, which has been split by a storm and which now forms a triangular arch over the ground. Then she walks under it. When they reach the stream, Melly touches the water and the wood turtle, which sits patiently on a rock. She treats it like a dog or cat. She touches the mud on her grandmother's snow boots, the corduroy of Ada's jacket, the stem and blossom of a waving wildflower, bright blue, the soggy leaf that falls on her shoulder, the bark of a huge maple. She reaches up into space as if she could touch the sky, which makes them all look up. It is the brightest, most perfect, blue. As they look at it, Melly traces each finger of her Aunt Ada's hand.

Later when they are back at the cottage for an afternoon nap, Emily tells her daughter that since she has been so good, she may sleep in the room with her grandmother. Ada's room is next to Emma's and she can hear Emma trying to put the child to sleep.

"You're lovely," Emma says. "Lovely. Not just because you're pretty, although you are, but that doesn't count, really. You're lovely because you help your mother carry groceries. I like a girl who knows how to help! That's a good thing. You're very small, but you can carry things already. What a perfect, perfect child you are."

For a long time Ada can't sleep, wondering if her mother feels her love, wondering if it is her lot in life to be unappreciated, to make her mother happy not because of anything in her, but because she can organize an event that brings her mother into contact with Emily and Melanie. She wonders what her mother said to her when she was a baby. Finally she drops off to sleep in the midst of worries that float to earth like the last of the autumn leaves.

The afternoon nap is interrupted prematurely by the visit of the owners who have come to see if everything is satisfactory. When Ada answers the door she is distracted from her conversation with Roger and Elaine because she can hear her mother grumbling about having been awakened.

"Are you warm enough?" Elaine asks. Her husband wants to know if Ada is good at building a fire.

"Fine," Ada declares.

Just as the couple is about to leave, Elaine turns and adds, "Hunters aren't bothering you, are they?"

"Hunters?" Ada tries to remember if she's heard any shots. "No," she says slowly, "I haven't been aware of anything."

"Okay. Good." Roger nods to his wife that they should go.

"They don't come up close, do they?"

"Yeah, they do. They come up pretty close."

"Thanks for telling us. We'll be careful."

Behind her, as she closes the door, Ada hears the others come into the room. She turns to see the adults each holding one of Melanie's hands. They are discussing the prices that Emma should charge for various items on the menu. They walk Melanie and talk for some time but do not include Ada in the conversation.

"I think it's starting to rain," Ada says finally. They look at her as if she is a stranger on a bus or in a park, making conversation out of the weather.

This is how things are in her family. By the time dark falls over the cabin, Ada feels very alone. Emily has been washing dishes and muttering to no one in particular that she is afraid Bob will have trouble finding the place. Melanie has been dragging kitchen chairs around in some pattern that to her is obviously not as random as it looks. Ada, sitting in the only kitchen chair still at the table, is reading the beginning of a novel over and over again, trying to concentrate. When Bob arrives, everybody moves. Melanie leaves the chairs in the middle of the floor, Ada puts her book down, Emily runs her wet hands through her hair a few times, and they all go to greet Bob. In the living room, Emma pokes her head out from under the afghan.

The cheering effect of the arrival of Emily and her daughter is easily cubed by Bob's effect on everyone. Bob lifts Melanie into the air, pretends to drop her, lifts her again, and then carries her around under his arm as if she is a satchel. Melanie cannot take her eyes off him, but all the others watch, too, and laugh as if Bob is tossing them about. When Bob puts Melanie down, she looks disappointed. When he greets the others, she retreats to the kitchen and peers out to see if he will follow her. Bob is good at teasing Melanie, pretending for a long time not to see her, making her work for his attention, making her suffer and wait and feel disappointment. Then he dives at her, hugs her and kisses her, lifts her, looks at her, talks to her. She cannot wait to play again. Emma, laughing, gets up to comb her hair.

"There are hunters in the woods," Ada tells Bob. "If you go out for a walk, be careful."

"I'm just going to sleep," he says. "I'm bushed."

He is tall and blonde, huskily built. His hairline is receding. He lies down in the spot vacated by Emma. Melanie climbs up onto his chest and Ada looks at them both for a long time, thinking how happy they look, noting how much alike they look, feeling glad the world seems so much lovelier than it did moments ago.

Ada just sits and looks and thinks. Franklin is not at all like her brother-in-law. Franklin is leaner, for one thing, and nervous. He would never toss a child into the air for fear of dropping or hurting the child. Well, maybe he would if he could practice for a while with something non-destructible. Franklin is a great one for practice. He is a dentist, has fine dexterity, yet still he practices at least once a week. His friends get all kinds of jokes out of that, but Ada often wishes he would relax and rest on his laurels.

People assume since Franklin is such a worrier and a practicer he is rehearsing a serious relationship with Ada that will one day be the real thing. But Ada knows this is not true because she has talked to him about it. He wants to marry some day, but he doesn't want to marry her. At least he doesn't think so. He keeps meaning to get around to dating other women, he says, but that doesn't ever seem to happen. At times Ada has tried to break away, but she always gets lonely and can't stick to it. And then Franklin feels bad, hugs her and kisses her, and although things never go further, a deadening sort of comfort overtakes them both.

In matters other than love, Franklin is a gem. He finds countless ways to do favors for Ada. He takes her car for servicing, helps her plant shrubs, brings her soup when she is sick. He would probably rake her leaves if she asked him. He always takes her out on her birthday and Christmas. Just this weekend, he is taking her mail inside, turning lights off and on. Once she came back from vacation to find a refrigerator full of food. He seems always to be looking for ways to love her. And she is used to him. Without him, she will be so completely alone.

On Sunday morning, Ada tries to figure out the menus for the day as she cleans the kitchen counter. She is the first up. Soon her mother shuffles in, still sleepy-looking, but now there is a healthy color in her face. She sits down. "Pour me a cup of coffee," she says.

Ada hesitates for a moment because she doesn't like her mother's tone. But she overcomes her resistance and pours a cup of coffee. "Do you like it here?" she asks.

"I do," Emma says. "I'm getting a lot of rest."

"Good. You look nice and rested. We can come back again some weekend."

Emma hesitates. "I guess so. I don't know if Emily can get away that easily though. And Bob. This was hard on them."

"They wouldn't have to come. I could bring you."

Emma makes a face as if the coffee is too hot, but the expression lingers. "I guess," she says.

Ada cannot escape it any longer. Here it is, a meanness, a punishment that puzzles her. And now she thinks of it, always has. "What is it, Mom?" she whispers. "Why are you angry with me?"

Emma gets up from the table and goes into the living room. Ada follows her, asking again, "What is it?"

She doesn't get an answer. The look on her mother's face frightens her, an anxious dark look that could lead to a heart attack. But Ada thinks she reads, "Because you're always bothering me," on her mother's face. She thinks better of asking her mother anything more and backs into the kitchen. She chooses a chair in the middle of the floor, one nobody put back when Melanie moved it. Like a dunce in a classroom, she works it through, over and over. It is not her imagination. Her mother behaves badly to her. It makes her sad. It makes her mad. Then her mother behaves badly to her because she is sad and mad. A cycle. It has always been like this. Ada has always tried hard to please her mother and has never succeeded. And if her mother moved in with her? Surely it would be worse. "It's not my fault," Ada tells herself. She sits in the kitchen and pounds this idea into her head. And once she's got that straight, another thought that she does not welcome comes to her, strong and clear: Franklin does not love her.

At nine o'clock on Sunday morning Ada does something that is very unusual for her. She decides to let them all fend for themselves. She dresses, just jeans and a sweatshirt, and leaves the house. She has not done much with her hair and she doesn't have any makeup on. "Perhaps someone will shoot me," she thinks hopefully as she walks into the woods. For hours and hours she walks, feeling awful. Bereft. Alone. At one point she sits on a rock and wonders what she will tell Franklin.

She knows eventually she will have to go back for her car. Perhaps the others will be gone. Perhaps not. But she hopes they will. And then she'll really be alone. That's what it's like, she taunts herself, when a girl leaves home for the first time. She doesn't even know if she can get back. She has followed the stream, watched the landmarks, but she's walked for so long she has no idea where she is. Yet there is something wonderful in that, a heady feeling. A thrill goes through her. Freedom.

Up ahead she sees a gas station and a market. There is nothing she needs, but she wants to buy something. At the market she chooses a cart, which she eventually realizes has a broken right front wheel. It turns inward like a wounded foot, making the cart impossible to push from behind. Ada moves to the front of it and drags it behind her. She practically crashes into a man with a full cart. The man wears a classic red and black hunter's shirt. He says a gravelly, "Hey, lady, why don't you learn how to drive?" Ada sees that he is very handsome. He has thick dark hair with a few flecks of gray and a thick beard. "I was just joking," he adds. It must be true.

His eyes are pleasant and bemused.

"I can't drive today," she says stupidly. "It's one of those days." The man disappears behind a shelf full of cereals and Ada drags the cart for a while choosing tomatoes and donuts from the counters. Then she goes to the checkout line. There her attention is caught by a child of two or three who is sitting in the cart in front of her. A harried man in a fuzzy cap and glasses, which he constantly and irritably readjusts, looks to be the boy's father. The boy is his father's opposite. He loves the world. In place of a toy, he has his father's checkbook, which he scribbles in with a red pen. He looks up occasionally and flirts with Ada. Yes, it is flirting. She has never seen a child quite like this. He has huge blue eyes and the well-fed richness of a Cupid or a boy-god. Even his dirty face speaks of privilege. Underneath everything—dirty face, tousled hair, chubby body, navy-blue down jacket—is laughter so deep that Ada falls into it. Already it is clear that this boy will cause great suffering to many women. Yet Ada cannot take her eyes off him. She is totally fascinated.

She finds herself performing for him, dipping her head down to catch his eyes, pretending to look away and then looking back, asking him what he is doing with the red pen and the checkbook. He laughs, of course. He laughs in answer to everything, a silent open-mouthed laugh, while he answers each look of Ada's, each gesture, with the cunning of one who knows his power.

Ada remembers where she saw this boy. In her mind. He was evoked once in a dance program that Franklin took her to in an Indian Temple newly built on a hilltop outside of Pittsburgh. The dancer, a woman, narrated each story before dancing it. She explained that one of her story-dances would be of a woman who left home one day on an ordinary errand and found herself confronted by the beautiful elusive boy-god Krishna. She fell immediately in love with him, so in love that she could think of nothing but capturing his attention. She danced for him. She plucked fruit from a tree and offered it. She tried to engage him in a game of catch. Finally he smiled at her. And then he ran away. When she lost him, her heart was broken. She ambled home, distracted and sad. Upon arriving home, she saw that her young son had disobeyed her and gone into the yard while she was gone. He sat on the ground eating handfuls of dirt. How angry she was. The sad girl had become a raging, reprimanding mother. The boy turned to her and in that instant she saw with amazement that the boy-god Krishna was incarnated in her very own son. His beauty melted her. She was smitten for life.

Ada watches the boy-god leave the supermarket. She pays the checker in a dream and tries to push her limping cart outside. The thick-haired man, standing in another checkout line, catches her eye and smiles.

"It's the cart," she says apologetically.

And back she walks through the woods, listening to the leaves crackle under her feet—a sound that fills up the air—listening for the answering tread of the man in the red plaid shirt, hearing the singing at the back of her head, a love call that makes her dizzy with longing for the elusive boy-god. She considers it remarkable, a gift, that she saw him so late in life and in such an unexpected place, while buying donuts and tomatoes, for no good reason at all.

THE ELEPHANT BOY

for Monty

It was junk day in Alice's neighborhood, and she, who had spent a lifetime accumulating burdens of one sort or another, moved methodically through her house dragging boxes behind her. Into the cartons went the little things—packets of letters twenty or thirty years old, crushed enamel boxes, posters that had never been framed and were turning yellow. In her mind, she marked the larger pieces that would go. There was the footstool, which was too low, too hard, and no longer pretty to look at, its embroidery tattered and almost sandy with age. The small cabinet with the broken hinge. She thought perhaps she should throw out the old daybed, which had been rescued from the debris of the farmhouse, repaired, and re-covered so many times. . . .

And then the phone rang. Nothing would convince her ever that the moment was accidental.

"Am I speaking to Alice Greer?" an unfamiliar man's voice asked.

She said that he was.

The man marveled at the ease of finding her. He told her he was Mohandas Thompson and asked if she remembered him.

Mohandas! And such a grown-up voice. But of course, he would be forty now.

He explained that he was in town on business. He estimated that he had three hours before he had to be at the airport. He went on in a reasonable, formal voice. Might he speak to her? Might he come take her out for an afternoon tea or a late lunch? "Or would you meet me for an early cocktail?" He laughed a rich, throaty laugh.

"Would you come to my house? Would *that* be possible?" Alice asked before she had thought about it. And before she could change her mind, he said he would be there in twenty minutes.

Mohandas turned from the phone booth. He had called to tell her his father had died. Her voice on the phone did not suggest she'd heard. And since fate had brought him to town on business, since he had found her name in the phone book, since she had answered the phone on the first ring, it seemed he should tell her in person. Yes, that seemed the thing to do. Had his father kept up a correspondence or any sort of relationship with her, he wondered, over the last twenty-five of the thirty years since they'd met? He'd seen no evidence but didn't know. Had she cared to know Leon during those years? Perhaps not.

Perhaps the news of his father's death would mean nothing to her, Mohandas thought. But his task, then, would be done.

Mohandas was American and of English-German background. He had been named after an Indian acquaintance of his parents. And then, at the age of ten, his parents had taken him off to live for over ten years in Bombay where he eventually attended the university. He spoke, even though he had been back in the States for some time, with an evenness of inflection that was not particularly American. And stranger than that vocal characteristic were his looks, a distillation of his father's looks, dark and Asian from the almond eyes to the heavy, straight hair. His was a mysterious heritage that could not be accounted for in his German or English ancestors. He even went, for convenience, by the name Matthew, but many people asked him leading questions about Japan or the Middle East or India or said things to him with a query in their looks as if they were trying to piece something together. And once they saw his real name written, they were utterly convinced he had Indian blood in him.

Alice had no time to spend on putting things right. Twenty minutes. She dragged two boxes from the living room to the back sunporch. Seeing herself in the little rattan-bound mirror on the wall, she decided to give up all efforts but showering to make herself ready. Her graying hair stood up in scattered, occasional question and exclamation points. She knew she was plain, the plain that comes of not noticing oneself for a long time. She knew she had grown old beyond her years. She knew, too, there was anger in her and wished she could wash it away as she could the sweat of the summer day's work of cleaning house.

As she stood in the shower, the old days passed before her. It couldn't be helped, given the surprise of the phone call, Mohandas' voice after thirty years.

She had asked him nothing. Why had she asked him nothing? When he arrived, she would ask about his business, his parents, his life. What life could the poor boy have had? Wasn't it a miracle that he had made it, somehow, through thirty more years after that summer?

They had all known each other thirty years ago—Alice, the boy, and his parents Leon and Julianna. For two summers, Mohandas had come close to driving them all crazy, fool—or was it that?—that he had been. And Alice, who was then not much past the age of twenty, had bloomed brightly and faded quickly.

Alice had gone to college poor. She had left a perpetually sad, defeated family of seven at home to slog along financially while she scraped out her university education with scholarships and a job in the staff cafeteria. Having had so many siblings to care for, clean for, she accepted a life of drudgery without thinking about it. She donned without complaint the limp blue uniform and surgical-style cap that she was ordered to wear behind the cafeteria line. Others whined about the drabness of the dress, an insult beyond the job, but Alice never minded. It was a job. And she figured she wasn't that good-looking anyway.

In truth, Alice was close to being beautiful, but she didn't know it. Through the years, some people had seen it in her and some hadn't.

One day, at the cafeteria, Alice had dished out a scoop of mashed potatoes and was dashing gravy across the plate when a man said, "You must be reviewing for an exam! You've removed yourself completely from this dreary cafeteria! That's for sure!" Alice had looked up to see a dark-skinned man whom she didn't know. His smile was condescending, his whole manner, she thought, arrogant. Her heart beat fast, but she simply asked him, "Peas or beans?" with a raise of the eyebrows that made her own face more arrogant than she could have guessed. What she'd seen in him, he saw in her, a way of getting above it all.

A year later she took a course in World Literature, and there was the man again. At first Leon seemed to lecture to everyone who sat in the huge hall but her. Later, only days later—perhaps it was the force of her receiving—he lectured only to her.

He told the class stories. One in particular had everything to do with the way these lives came together. She could still see and hear how he told it.

"Many of the great stories of the world are stories about marriages," he began. He moved away from the podium and talked about the gods as if they were neighbors. "Zeus philandered, you recall, and Hera went on rampages. She punished his conquests in one way or another, not always directly. Last week we discussed the way poor Heracles bore the brunt of the punishment directed toward Alcmena." He ran his hands through his hair and shook his head at the plight of Heracles. "A slightly different version of the marriage tale is told in Hindu literature. It is the story of the making and saving of Ganesha." Here he nodded and repeated the name. "Ganesha."

Students wrote down the name. Leon sat on the edge of the desk and began in a once-upon-a-time voice to pull them into the story. Alice remembered this. The class, almost to a person, closed or put aside notebooks and listened like children.

"One day, Parvati, Shiva's wife, wanted to take a bath!" Leon said. "And she wanted to take her bath in peace! She told her guard to make sure she was not disturbed. But when Shiva himself came toward her chamber, the guard thought it was not his duty to keep him out. Not Shiva! Not her husband and the greatest of men! The greatest of gods!

"Parvati, however, did not agree. When she wanted peace, she wanted peace. 'I need a better guard,' she said. 'One who recognizes my word as primary.' So, from her own body she created a boy, a handsome strong boy. 'My son,' she said to him, 'let no one in unless I say you may.' The boy took her at her word and barred the door, even to Shiva! Shiva was astounded. When he tried to enter anyway, the boy hit him. At first Shiva was patient. He sent counselors to remove the boy in order to clear his way. But the boy would not budge because Parvati had said again that no one, not even Shiva, was to enter without her permission. Finally Shiva sent his men to fight the boy."

As she toweled her hair dry, Alice thought about these first moments of knowing Leon. What a memory she had. But for a pause or a word here or there, what she recalled might have been a recording of the classroom event. She'd thought about it before, but today she saw and heard with clarity: "David slew Goliath, Heracles performed difficult labors, and the boy, Parvati's boy, fought off an army of Shiva's men."

Yes, that's exactly how he would sound.

He was young, Parvati's boy. He was one against many. She remembered that. But he won. Even though other deities gathered around Shiva and tried to help.

"Do you think that Brahma with his age and dignity could move the boy?" Leon had asked. "No, not even his white beard could budge him. And so Shiva declared war. The goal was no longer to push past the boy or to remove him from his post or to persuade him to leave, but to destroy him."

Twenty minutes had passed in a flash. The doorbell rang.

Mohandas peered through the glass into the living room but could see nothing. He felt curious and excited. He wore a cool summer suit in taupe and cream tones. In the glass of the door he saw that his tie, of Indian silk in brown and red, had slid toward his left lapel, and he straightened it.

In the bedroom, Alice pulled her dress over her head. It was a tent-like affair in pink and peach canvas-like cotton, a style that hid the extra rolls of weight around her middle but did nothing to flatter her. "He's here," she said to herself. "He's here." But what she pictured in her mind was the father as he was back then, not the son.

What she found at the door was a combination of her memories of the father and the son as well as a person who was startlingly neither. On the other side of the glass Mohandas laughed at the way she looked at him. He knew he had grown handsome. It was implicit in the way people talked to him. His wife Marianne told him often that he was good-looking and not just to her.

Mohandas must be thinking, Alice whispered to herself, that I have not improved. I've aged so much. But he smiled at her in a way that made it not matter.

She opened the door to him. "No," he was saying as if they'd been in the midst of a conversation. "I'm not a fat, obnoxious boy! I'm sure, though, that's how you've thought of me."

And it was true. She had always remembered him as he had been at ten.

"You stole money from me once," she told him in confirmation. "I didn't have much money to begin with. And when I caught you and yelled at you, you thundered down the steps, bellowing as if I were in the wrong. I remember that."

But for some reason beyond reason, maybe just time, the memory made her smile. He seemed to find this a perfectly ordinary first exchange between them.

Mohandas was easily at home anywhere. He stood in Alice's living room with his hands clasped lightly, and he let her look at him. "Where can we sit and talk?" he asked.

Since they were in the living room and he did not naturally move to a couch or a chair, Alice answered,

"Wherever you like. Look around." Her heart raced in a way it hadn't for ages. Mohandas walked straight back to the sunporch and moved two boxes out of the way of a rattan chair.

"Ah," he said. "Let's sit in here."

"May I get you a drink? Or tea? Or, let me think, coffee?"

"Something cool would be nice. Juice, if you have it."

"Lemonade?"

"Just the thing."

Mohandas looked around him and smiled. When he was alone he often thought about his wife, especially about things she said. Her voice stayed with him. While he waited for Alice to return with the lemonade, his wife Marianne came to mind. She had encouraged him to come here, although he would have come without encouragement. She knew all about the old days, about the affair between Alice and his father. Mohandas had even told his mother that he was planning to look Alice up. Julianna had given a curt, perhaps sage, nod. She had not said, "Don't go." And now he was here. It made him smile.

In the kitchen, Alice remembered once more Mohandas, the fat boy, nothing but trouble. Who was he now? Not the same person! Had Leon changed, too? Mohandas' father had been so insistent and unscrupulous a seducer that even the memory of him made a knot in her stomach. Who was Leon now? And Mohandas' mother, Julianna, had been a cobweb-haired Miss Havisham in the making. What had become of them all after thirty years?

Alice returned with the glasses of lemonade. "What is it you do?" she asked. "You said you were in town on business."

"Banking."

"If they've got you traveling, it must be banking at a very high level."

"High enough, yes. And your work?"

Alice explained that oddly enough, she had become an administrator at the Fulbright Office. 'Oddly enough' because the Fulbright Foundation had once paid her salary, the years she worked for his father. But he didn't question the phrase and she let it pass.

"I came to tell you something," he began. "I think you may not have heard. About a half-year ago, my father died. I thought you might want to know."

The first feeling that hit Alice was relief, like a sigh escaping. She couldn't have explained it and she was ashamed of feeling it, relief at someone's death, but there it was, that's what she felt. She blushed to think Mohandas might see it. "I hadn't heard," she said finally. "I'm sorry. What did he die of?"

"His heart. He'd had several attacks. And then a final one."

"Only sixty-five," she said. "Did he have a good life?"

Mohandas shifted in his seat. Uncomfortable feelings welled in him. "I don't think so. He was not a very good man, and I believe—many people think I'm very stupid by the way—that happiness and goodness go hand in hand. His financial dealings were always a little shady. He was full of promises that he never kept. He was kind or cruel depending on his most selfish needs. And not least by far, I believe he treated women very badly. No, I don't think his life was good. Or happy."

"Oh, I agree with you! About goodness! . . .and about your father." Alice was surprised at the passion in her voice. She was so grateful to this man for being able to say these things that she wanted to hug him, to tell him things she had told no one.

"But I loved him very much anyway. I can't explain it," Mohandas said. "I just did."

"Yes."

Mohandas saw that Alice's eyes were brimming with tears. He had not forgotten her in thirty years. He sat now in her sunroom, seeing the stillness of the trees outside, the fact that the marigolds did not so much as nod, and he knew what she was feeling. He understood her.

"He was so intelligent," Alice said. "And so unhappy."

"And lazy, too," he reminded her.

"Yes."

"Oh, yes."

Nothing had come of the Fulbright project except that her life had been radically altered. No book. No articles. And if wisdom had come of it, where was the wisdom? "I want to find traces of the Ganesha legend in Western literature," Leon Thompson had explained to her. "And I need a research assistant. I can't pay royally, but it can't be much worse than the cafeteria money."

She had accepted the job. She would have eaten sandpaper if he had asked her to, and he saw that. Taking the job meant spending summers at what Leon sarcastically referred to as his country home. The second home was a ramshackle farmhouse in which Julianna Thompson could be heard puttering around from morning to night without ever clearing the mess or producing much to eat. Leon explained that he planned to renovate the place as soon as he had enough money. The place never got renovated. The book never got written.

Alice thought at first that living in the farmhouse was like camping: earthy, simple, temporary. Then she took to calling her quarters "Little Calcutta" because it conjured for her the constant dirt and crowding of an exotic ghetto. Later she thought of the whole place as more like a desert setting, something out of literature, away from time and place. It was her own life with him, removed from the reality of his marriage, her peers, her youth, fun, that she was responding to.

"Why don't you leave her?" she had cried to him one day in the office, the self-contained quarters on the third floor where she stayed. Her own stove, her own bathroom, the day-bed (which she still owned!), a lockable door.

"Look at her," he said. "How can I?"

And Julianna did seem mad, in a distracted way, incapable of taking care of herself. But then Leon mesmerized people into going against themselves. Alice thought about this often but couldn't find a way out.

How many times Leon dragged Alice into the closest little town to shop for supplies, only to let her witness intense whispering and an exchange of understanding looks between him and Lydia, a cheerful, angular woman who ran the shop. He would let Alice see that he wasn't hers. Then he would make the next trip into town alone. Who would put up with such a thing? And yet they all did. He could talk them into a dream. And the farmhouse arrangement? His family quarters on the first two floors, Alice in an apartment-office on the third. Surely Julianna must have wondered at the long hours spent in the heat of the attic. Surely he knew Julianna would see Alice's skin, flushed with guilt, anger, the fiery determination of youth. Surely it was done to torture, to say, 'See, I belong to no one.' Or was that simply what Alice came to feel?

She had tried to leave once, and he had sworn that he loved her, that he'd never loved anyone as he loved her. And she had stayed, begging him to make things right, to leave Julianna. The next day, or two days later, she had gone to the city with him, to the library, where they encountered, quite by accident (it seemed), a woman who was Leon's colleague. The two professors then enacted a version of the scene in the village store. Alice stood in the stacks, wanting to be invisible, while they murmured and whispered a conversation, snatches of which she could hear, about their plans to meet in two weeks. The man couldn't stop. He thought he was Zeus.

The memories came to Alice in a fury of images, as quickly as her guest swirled ice cubes and took two or three drinks. She couldn't hide the fact that anger was stirring in her, and so she said, "Perhaps I shouldn't tell you this, but he also treated me very badly."

"I know that. I don't see how you could help hating him."

The lemonade glass was cool in her hands. "I have hated him. And I never wanted to feel anything but love."

"You were young," he said. "You were just a girl."

"Thank you. But I no longer think of that as an excuse."

He gave huge heaving nods of understanding.

At the time, in a welter of mixed feelings, Alice had attached many of the bad ones to Mohandas. She had despised him as one despises a fool when there is no room or time for folly. They had all used Mohandas this way. His mother had griped at him all the day long. His father had exploded with threats and rages. Alice would lie for long hours beside Leon discussing his hopeless son, the beast of a boy who stole money from her, hit her window with a stone from a slingshot, ran at her with all the force of his body, came into her room when she forgot to lock the door, and more, worse. Much of his anger came out as stupidity, recklessness. It seemed to be constant and without a target. Nobody thought he would grow up to be all right. Had he?

"How much you've changed," she said. "You seem so calm." They sat looking out at her yard as if they had always sat there like this. "You used to do awful things. You killed a cat once. Do you remember?"

Mohandas did, and he didn't like to think of it. It gave him a pain around his heart to think of it.

He had been awful. He remembered absorbing the miseries around him and lashing out. A destructive fat boy. What a miracle that anyone had cared about him, that he had grown up beyond it all, he thought. And perhaps he wouldn't have, couldn't have, without Alice to look at him and through him the way she had. Once he had started the car and driven it right into the farmhouse. The car bashed part of the dining room wall in and his mother screamed, a sound that came from her depths. And for days his father tried to reconstruct the dining room wall while Mohandas found other things to take apart.

One day he decided that the house wanted to fall down. Needed to fall down. For weeks he sawed and pounded. He imported logs infested with carpenter ants, he dragged a heavy bag of cement onto the roof and worked away making noises like thunder until the earth began to move under them or so it seemed. It was sections of flooring. They had fled, all of them, in the car, frightened that the roof or upper floors would fall on their heads. After that they had moved to India and left Alice behind. Once, years later, when he went back with his father to rescue pieces of furniture, he saw the house collapsed like jagged bones in settled dust. They were never sure what had finally done it.

He thought of these things as he looked into the garden. When he looked away from the garden he caught a glimpse of himself in Alice's rattan-bound mirror: trim, suited, sober, and a perfect-looking citizen. He felt that he was very fortunate, and it made him chuckle.

Alice wondered what Mohandas was thinking.

"I'm very sorry for my part in your family's unhappiness," she said. "You must have hated me."

"On the contrary. I think I loved you very much. But you must have hated me, and I don't blame you."

Alice shook her head and pursed her lips. The phrase that came to her was, "On the contrary." She didn't want to say what he'd said. But it was true that she hadn't hated him ever, hadn't even thought him demented. She had hated some part of herself. He was her struggle, her "made son," her adopted boy. She loved him. Then and now. Had wanted him to grow up right. And the miracle—what else could it be—had happened. He had risen up out of the debris with his soul intact. Could it be?

"Your father and I talked about you more than anything else," she told him. "It was as if you were our son. We talked about you more than we talked about the research." No, she thought. Instead of the research. In place of it. "Your father looked everywhere in literature for stories of Ganesha. He was a boy who was destroyed and put back together again. Your father thought of this as an important story of transformation."

"I remember."

"I think the whole time, he was thinking of you."

"He wished that I was better than I was."

"Something like that."

"Funny."

Alice felt that her whole life had been leading to this moment, this afternoon with the quiet, handsome man who was better than he had been, sitting in her sunroom, drinking lemonade. She looked around her. The room was a mess and so was she, but it really didn't matter. Mohandas smiled at her.

He wondered if she'd had any love in her life. There was the garden. And a rosiness in her cheeks. There was life here. And things. Her house was full of things.

"What's all this?" he asked, nodding toward the boxes. "Are you planning to move?"

"Junk day. I have to have these things on the front curb by tomorrow morning."

"Let me help!" He stood and handed her his lemonade glass. "Put me to work."

"Really? You're all dressed up."

"Really. It doesn't matter."

"Okay. All right." She pointed to the cabinet and the footstool. "I'll get us more lemonade." She stood for a moment and watched him. He left his suit jacket on and lifted things easily. When she went into the kitchen she realized that for years she had lived with old things, reminders of the days with Leon, left them around her even when she no longer wanted them. On the day she decided to throw them away Mohandas appeared. How strange. She would make sure he took out the daybed. How stupid of her to have kept it all these years. But when she came back into the room, he was already carrying out the bottom mattress. She put down the lemonade and carried out the covers and pillows. Together they walked back for the frame. They each took an end and carried it out. Their progress through the house was so smooth, she said, "We're old hands at this."

He said, "Now, what else? Put me to work while I'm here."

"Nothing. Small things. I'll take care of them tonight."

"Whatever you say."

They settled back into their chairs and took up their glasses of lemonade. "Can you stay for dinner?"

"I can't. I have to be at the airport. I've promised to be home for a late dinner with my wife and my daughters. Did I tell you I have two daughters?"

"No!" It was as if she had grandchildren, a secret treasure, only now revealed.

Mohandas loved to describe his family. "My wife Marianne," he began, "is small and dark. She is thirty-four years old. Very fit. She loves clothes and has all kinds, styles, I mean. Sometimes she's very sporty. Sometimes she dresses like a country girl. She's very pretty."

He loves her! Alice thought. He loves her. She tucked this away as further evidence of his grace.

"My daughters are ten and seven. The ten-year-old is so smart we're all frightened of her!" He laughed. "Not really. But what a determined child! She takes dancing lessons. She practices for four hours a day. Piano, the same. I wonder if she'll always be the best at everything. No. Of course no one can. But her disappointments are still in the future."

"She must be extraordinary!"

"She's okay, for now, Cynthia is."

"Cynthia."

"Yes. And the little one is Laurie. She doesn't try very hard at all, but she does everything reasonably well anyway. Laurie is tiny like her mother. And she loves jokes. She collects them." Alice smiled as if she could see these people, and Mohandas appreciated her interest.

In fact he wished he could stay and talk to her longer. He saw that she was very alone. If only someone cared for her. She had once been beautiful. She had once taken him on a picnic, even though he was nobody's friend then, fat and miserable as he was. She had leaned against a tree and told him stories all the afternoon long. The one about Ganesha she told him many times. It had affected him deeply. He could still see how her face had been, full of feeling, especially when she talked about the forces that came against the boy and how he remained valiant, until only by the treachery of the gods, by deceit, could he be killed. Even then, the queen had insisted that he live again.

Now, here he was, seeing Alice again. Her youth was gone. But there was still that hopeful look about her. He wished he could do something for her.

Alice asked, "How is your mother? Is she well?"

"More than well. She opened a bookstore two years ago. It's been the happiest thing she ever did." He looked at his watch and stood up to go. "She never blamed you, you know."

"No, I didn't know. Thank you for telling me."

"I'm going to have to go now."

They walked together to her front door. He kissed her on the cheek and said good-bye. She watched him swaying with a deep happiness as he walked down her sidewalk to his rented car. She thought, "He is a miracle. A miracle."

He was thinking all kinds of things—that he would tell his mother how deeply Alice had suffered, more deeply than she knew herself. He thought domestic thoughts, too, about the last party he had gone to with Marianne and his secret knowledge that she was on the brink of an affair. He would return home, and later tonight he would kiss her and talk and talk about the visit with Alice. He would tell Marianne how old Alice had grown, what a nice woman she was, and the two thoughts together would amount to how much waste there was in the world. He would tell her his philosophy, that there was only love in the world, only love and reactions to love, only commitment and strains against commitment, but in the end only love and commitment. That was all there was. Just love. And you never could betray it, even when you thought you could. Or maybe he was just stupid.

Alice cried in a quiet sort of way for the rest of the day. She had many of the same thoughts about herself, and felt, too, that she had grown old wastefully. It seemed, oddly, that the few relationships she had had in the thirty years after Leon had been like extramarital affairs and that she had been married to him the whole time. And angry with him. And, today, sad for him. She found she was crying because he'd died without ever being happy.

Yes, amazing, but she could hear Leon speaking as clearly as if she'd tape-recorded it: "The boy was beset on all sides. But he fought bravely. Vishnu came at him on a bird and occupied all his energies. While he fought Vishnu, Shiva snuck up behind him, unfair, deceitful Shiva, and without warning he cut off the boy's head. All the warriors gathered around, quiet, stunned, looking at the dead boy. Shiva was suddenly sorry for what he had done. He had killed the boy. And Parvati, well, she vowed nothing less than death for the whole lot of them, all the armies of Shiva. She called up terrible forces to destroy them until they all cried to her for mercy. 'What can we do to appease you?' they asked. Her only answer was that her son must be brought back to life. 'Very well,' Shiva said. 'Cut off the head of the first animal you see and fix it to the boy's body.' Why this worked, merging man and beast, we don't know. But Shiva was sure of it. The first animal to appear was an elephant. Which the men killed. And they fitted the head to the boy's body!"

Around the classroom there had risen a chorus of titters and guffaws. One of the texts contained a drawing of the ridiculous creature.

"You laugh," Leon had said. "But Parvati didn't laugh and she was a great goddess. She held the boy, embraced him, called him son. And then Shiva accepted him as an honored son, Ganesha, worthy of worship. A name to be reckoned with. Ganesha became known as the queller of obstacles. You laugh because you haven't yet thought about the beauty of the elephant and the dignity of the—to you, at this point, foolish-looking—elephant boy."

The whole class had become silent. Alice had fallen in love with Leon at that moment because she had understood that he was seeking something, a way of becoming better than he was.

THINGS PROGRESS

*H*arrison wants to know what my father did for a living. It's our third date and I'm already in love with him.

"Things progress," I say. "First he owned one bar, then two, then three."

"You must have been comfortable." We are walking into Three Rivers Stadium to a Pirates' game. People jostle us and several boys try to sell us tickets. I can hardly hear, let alone think. But comfortable is not the right word, in any sense. "No," I yell back. "It didn't work that way." Through the gates and into the crush on the escalator, I add, my face somewhere in the small of Harrison's back, eye to eye with his faded blue polo shirt, "He didn't tend bar, not most of the time. He was the atmosphere. People came to see him, like coming for a drink."

Harrison holds our tickets out so any roaming official might see we are legitimate. He nods as if he's heard me. His face is bright and excited about baseball. This is how I like to see him, sandy hair slightly mussed, casual clothes, an expectant look. A boy on a bike.

The men in the stands—oh, they are everywhere, with their big bellies, their beers, and their sad faces—seem to

*have been sent as a reminder of my father. How he was in the
middle years, somewhere between the Elias Grill days and the
Elias Bar days.*

For years there was just the Elias Grill. These were the
good days. My father walked from home to the bar, every
morning, past the closely placed houses, some wooden, many
of the newer ones covered with siding, a few good old brick
homes like our own. He thought there was nothing like red
brick, pleasant-looking and sturdy. If, on his walk, he saw a
woman sweeping her porch or a man getting into a car, he said
hello. He believed in friendliness, but oddly he didn't know
the names of many of our close neighbors, and he avoided
conversations with them. Distant friendliness appealed to
him. He grew into a role. His girth expanded, his hairline
receded, and his hair thinned on top so that his highly colored
balding skull became a target for teasing.

"Your shiny crown," the customers would say. "I know
I've got to listen up when I see that crown." They called him
King Andrew and he radiated benevolence.

"Were they neighborhood bars?"

*"The first one was. You could tell the time of day by the
regulars."*

"I know the kind of place you mean."

*"To be a regular, you had to have a shortened name or a
nickname. I remember Hymie, Fumie, and Macky-O. Oh,
and Pinky."*

Harrison gestures toward the field. "Spanky. Bobby Bo."

In my mind, my father laughs. He goes to the cash register, a beautiful thing with brassy embossed keys. When he
punches one, a number pops up behind the glass and a bell
rings.

"Dingdong," Fumie, an enormous blonde man, bellows.
He has the stick-straight hair of his East-European background
flattened further under a cap with a bill. "Master's home.
Everybody behave."

My father counts what's in the till and then reads the tiny
white slip of paper, which tells who still owes him money.
Soon he will get nickels and dimes and quarters from a niche
under the floorboards in the kitchen, a niche that can only be

gotten to by going halfway down the steps to the dimly lighted, dank, earthen-floored cellar. No matter how difficult he makes it to get to the money, there is always some missing. He takes note of it, but says nothing.

"Have you hit a million yet?" Mack O'Brien asks. This is no reference to the lottery—just an astronomical figure nobody can even imagine.

"Not quite, Macky-O," my father answers. "Macky-O, you'll be the first to know."

"If I buy you a drink, will you share your first million with me?"

The bar is a long, well-used slab of mahogany wood with circular stains. From down at the other end of it, Hymie yells, "What the hell, I offered first, what about my cut of the million?"

My father nods down to Hymie and makes an okay-circle with his fingers.

A glass of whiskey appears at my father's spot at the bar, the third stool from the kitchen side. If the place were really crowded, my father would go behind the bar and serve, too.

He was different with the customers than with our neighbors. He knew every name. He knew that Macky-O was really named Mackenzie O'Brien, that his wife's name was Angela, and that she was Italian. That Fumie, Frank Uenta, was violent, hit co-workers and his children. Fumie needed a lot of talking to. And that Hymie, John Hyman, had been impotent for years and his wife was banging the delivery man from the Harris and Boyer bread truck.

My father hoists the shot glass containing the drink he doesn't want. But he drinks the whiskey, a communion with the men who have waited for him. A light fire traces its way down his body, whispering a sweet message to close his eyes for a moment. And as the day wears on, as he buys almost as many drinks as are bought by others (because essentially he cannot bring himself to take anyone's money), he will also have many drinks bought for him and will close his eyes in communion a great many times.

*"A drinker?" Harrison asks. It seems we are surrounded
by them, big men, big drinkers. "Did he die of it?"*

*The game is beginning. "By the time he died, everything
was wrong. Probably the answer is yes."*

In the film-memory that comes to me (it slips by fast, before I know it's begun, like the video-summaries on the
scoreboard), I am with my mother, sister Genevieve, and
brother Andrew, and we are on a vacation in Ohio.

My father calls Ohio, and the relatives put my mother on
the phone. She is telling him he sounds slurry. I see myself,
listening, worried.

I get on the phone and say, "Couldn't you drive out and
see us?"

He laughs at me but after he hangs up, he calls right back
and says yes, a drive will help. And the next day he is in Ohio
to drive us back to Johnstown.

"You'd better never leave me," he says to my mother in
the car on the way home. "I don't think I'd make it."

"Whatever made you think of that?" She turns to the
three of us (I am in the film and out of it at the same time)
lined up in the back seat, passing a bottle of orange soda down
the line. I am explaining that I and Genevieve on the ends
should get two swigs in fairness because baby Andy in the
middle took a swig each time the bottle went past.

My mother says, "We'll never leave Daddy, will we?"

And, of course, that's the problem in a nutshell.

We scramble over each other to hug our father from
behind, to kiss his cheeks, to pat his shoulders, coo in his ears.
Send breaths of orange soda wafting toward him. He looks as
if he is going to cry.

"So you love me?" My mother asks.

"What do you want? A neon sign?"

Just before Thanksgiving the Moose Club held its annual
dance. One year they went.

My father surveyed himself in the mirror. He was aging,
while my mother remained lithe and beautiful. I hung at their
bedroom door as they dressed. I could see his heart ached.

"Don't look too good," he teased, "or I'll lose you to the bread man."

"What?"

"Harris and Boyer."

"Why?" My mother slipped on the black velvet skirt of the suit she would wear.

"Or the mailman."

"Aaach."

"What?"

"He's a sourpuss." She buttoned the black velvet jacket, which was cut to show her shape. It had a low plunging V neckline.

"There's always the milkman," he said.

"No," she sang as she fastened a rhinestone necklace shaped to follow the V of her suit jacket. "I'd rather have you."

He looked at her in amazement.

On the way out of the bedroom they saw me hovering at the door. "You look beautiful," I told her.

She looked at him for confirmation and he said, "Yeah. . . nifty," and "Okay by me."

Up to this point, my mother seemed contented. For one thing, she would look at our house and say it was a palace. "It has ten rooms," she would say. If she counted everything—the bathroom, powder room, kitchen—it did. "Our house is just like in the movies," she said. Although she hardly ever saw a movie after she got married, the idea of movies seeped into her life, part of the collective unconscious, like politics. The glamorous thing just then was to live in a house with a rose bush outside and sun streaming through paned glass windows. My mother cleaned every little window of the sun parlor, every little pane around the windows. "There are two hundred sixty-two windows in there!" she loved to say. It thrilled her to call a room a powder room, another a sun parlor, another a breakfast room. For a long time my mother didn't say *living room*; she said *parlor*.

She scrubbed it and polished it. Sometimes she stayed up all night and cleaned. My father didn't notice the changes, and she was hurt.

When I ran down for breakfast, I would say, "You washed the curtains!" or "You pinned them back with these little ruffles!" or "You waxed the floors! How beautiful they look!" Still, she would rather have heard it from my father. He was drifting farther and farther away.

The Pirates start out well: three up and three down and are about to go up to bat. "All right!" Harrison applauds. He grabs my hand and kisses it. This is the role he has taken with me, the crazy romantic who will change my life, and I don't mind it. But then he asks, "Did your father have a nickname?"

"No. . . .Oh, sometimes Big Daddy."

"Conjures machine guns."

Spanky slips and falls. The crowd mutters. I watch another film-memory, showing Harrison only a few clips.

"Once my father said, 'Don't answer the phone today. Or the door.' It was a Saturday, all of us children at home."

Everybody sniffling from colds. Outside, a bitter February gloom covers everything. The snow is dirty and lumpy. The sky looks like a five-o'clock-evening sky from early morning on. An occasional shout from outdoors pierces the air, and there is the steady hum of the television, a new acquisition. *My Friend, Flicka* is on. Andy wheedles, "Get me a hunk of bread, Helen, please."

"My mother told me, 'Keep everybody occupied.'"

While I buttered the bread at the counter, I asked, "But who are we hiding from?"

"I don't know."

I was angry at knowing so little, because I was ready to play Nancy Drew. I wanted to save my family, if only I knew how or from what.

"My mother used to rely on me for difficult things. Once, while she was washing clothes in the basement, she moved a basket and found a dead rat near the drain. She called for me. And I scrambled down the stairs and . . . and I took it all in. With me standing there, she felt able to scrape the rat onto a shovel with a broom, to dump the rat onto a spread of newspapers, and to take it out to the garbage. I was an important ingredient in coping."

"How did it get in here?" I ask when my mother gets back to the basement.

"I don't know. Through the drain?"

"Everything is so clean. . . ."

She breaths a grateful, "It is, isn't it?"

"The rat made some sort of mistake," I tell her.

"On the Saturday on which no one was supposed to answer the phone or the door, the phone kept ringing, of course. My brother Andy wanted to know why we couldn't answer. He thought maybe one of his friends was trying to invite him over."

Harrison turns reluctantly away from the game and asks me, "He was in the rackets?"

I don't know. It's not something I can give a definite answer to. "Who knows? Something mysterious, maybe the numbers."

That Saturday was an odd day. Genevieve dusted the table, and she dusted the phone, which kept ringing. "Isn't this fun?" she said in her sly sarcastic way.

My mother set to baking bread.

Suddenly, before anyone could stop him, Andy slipped on his coat and opened the front door just as a man appeared there, ready to knock.

"A man wants to see Dad!" Andy called out. I ran from upstairs where I'd gone to the bathroom towards the front door and saw him. Then I looked into the kitchen. My mother stood frozen at the sink.

I went to the front door. The man who stood there was large, square, his overcoat adding extra squareness and bulk. "I'm looking for your father." He consulted a piece of paper. "Andrew Elias."

"He's not here," I said.

"Where might he be?" the man asked.

"He's in Akron. You know where that is?"

"Yes, Miss." The man stood there for a while.

I stared at him. "Do you need a map? We might have one."

"No, thank you," he said. And he left.

I walked steadily past Genevieve who was clutching a dust cloth at the archway of the dining room, past Andy who now hesitated half-way up the stairs and into the kitchen. My mother stood at the sink, shaking. "Go into the parlor," she said. "Call the bar. See if Dad's there."

"What should I say?"

"Call me if you get him."

Vincent Ambrosia said my father wasn't there. I said, "Thank you. Would you tell him when he comes in that his daughter called and that she's in Akron."

I went to the sink and put my arms around my mother's waist, and I squeezed so hard that my mother said, "Watch it!" She was pregnant with Pamela then.

The man never came back. I told my father at suppertime that I had sent the man packing to Akron.

Things progress. My father came home one day in the fall of 1955 and announced that he was buying a second liquor license and a second establishment. "It just came along," he said.

"Will we be rich then?" Andy asked seriously.

"Oh, yeah!" my father answered in high spirits. "We'll be top of the heap!" But the face he made afterwards, a burlesque comic's lift of the eyebrows, warned us to expect nothing different in the way of finances. My father paused at the coat closet, disturbed, "What do you want that you don't have? If I should get rich some day, what would you like?"

"A baseball bat."

"A new winter coat!" my mother answered promptly.

"A transistor radio," I decided.

Genevieve asked for more time. She couldn't think what she wanted.

Pamela, even at three, knew to say, "Nothing. Don't need nothing."

At Christmas time, we all got what we'd asked for except my mother who got money to buy a coat instead of the coat itself. She put the money between two cups in the kitchen hutch and used it when regular funds ran low.

The Elias Grill, which my father owned before he married, was only five blocks from home and like an extension of home. The hot dogs rolled around on their machine. The neighbors drifted in and took the same seats everyday. They carried their lunch boxes with them, full or empty, depending upon which direction they were going, and if it was homeward, they often carried a loaf of bread or a quart of milk bought on the way. Their wives called the bar and asked for them, sometimes yelled for them.

The second place, the Elias Bar was farther from home in every way. When my mother and I went shopping, we had to transfer two times on trolleys and then walk several blocks to get to it. It was dark inside. The men who drank there were quieter, more often than not strangers to each other, alone in their thoughts. At the end of a row of rotting storefronts, the Elias Bar was not, and could not be made, bright or attractive.

The men at The Elias Grill called out and hooted, "Hello, gorgeous," and "Hey, baby," and "Isn't Andrew a lucky son-of-a-bitch-excuse-my-English-lucky-son-of-a-gun," when they saw my mother. "What did the son-ma-bitch—excuse me ladies—son-ma-gun do to deserve such a looker?" The men at the Elias Bar just stared, stared so hard that my mother said to me, "It makes me shiver, the way they look. Ugh. Creeps."

With the purchase of and burden of the second place, my father, already heavy, gained more weight. When he pushed the recliner to an upright position or hoisted himself out of it, he moved with more difficulty. His voice sagged when he said, "Hey! What's up!" to whichever one of us approached his chair. Once when Andy asked for money for a Little League outfit, seven-fifty—or nine dollars if he got his name sewed on—my father said, "Sure, boy," and heaved the chair up so he could reach into his back pocket where he kept a wad of bills, mostly ones, folded over in half. The wad was smaller than ever. Still he had a flair when he asked, benignly, "Tenner do it?" and pulled a ten-dollar bill from the outside of the packet.

After my father bought the second place and distanced himself, becoming a little more like the silent nameless men in the new bar, my mother lost her temper often and alarmingly, never at my father but at things and at me. Once, when I went to the basement looking for a clean blouse, I found my mother sobbing, throwing wet clothes, heavy and unmanageable with the weight of water, into a basket a full five feet away. Some pieces fell on the floor, others draped half in and half out of the basket. Frightened by this odd basketball practice, I ran to my mother and tried to talk to her. "What happened? What is it?" But she shook me off and slapped me. Then, because I stood there stunned, she hit me again and again, her forearm to my face and shoulders, saying, "Get out! Leave me alone."

"But. . . ."

"Get!" She stamped her foot at me, as if I were a stray animal that had made its way into the yard.

As I scrambled up the steps I could hear my mother sobbing.

Once I said I wanted to use my milk money to go somewhere and that I would be home later than usual.

"What for? Where?" my mother wanted to know.

"Downtown. A lot of the kids go. They use their milk money for the trolley."

"Who goes?" she asked, in curious not-blaming tones.

I named several of the girls from the neighborhood. I mentioned Renee.

"She was illegitimate," my mother said, not for the first time, and she added, as she usually did, "They have more life, more spirit. That's how it goes. They have. . . feeling. They move."

My heart beat hard as I gathered my books and started out the door.

"Here," my mother said. She dug into the cup and produced forty cents. "Don't skip the milk."

After school, I stood alone at the trolley stop, no friends around, no would-be shoppers to accompany me. Again and again, I went over the mental map of downtown, the streets I would take when I walked to my father's second place, the way I had done with my mother at the end of our shopping trips. Shopping. That was only a ruse. "If only he is still there; if only he hasn't left yet," I kept saying to myself. I had to get my father alone.

Main and Market to Main and Franklin. How poor and dirty-looking everything was. I walked past blank-looking and badly kept buildings. What was in them? Offices? Warehouses? The people who walked the streets were slower and blanker, too. The Elias Bar was at the very edge of town, a gray place.

When I walked into the bar, the familiar smells of damp wood, stale beer, fresh beer, whiskey, and strong cleaning solvent greeted me. I coughed from the heavy lingering layer of cigarette smoke, which like a cloud floated toward me. The television droned. I stood awkward and alone at the door, because the whole thing struck me strangely. I felt like an intruder, and suddenly I wanted to leave. I wanted to fetch my father out of there, although in my imagination, my meeting with him would take place right there, at a back booth. I'd imagined us soberly twisting our glasses on their damp circles on the table between us as I talked and he listened. But my eyes, now accustomed to the dark, allowed me to scan the bar, to look as I suspected I was being looked at. My father was not there.

"Hey, there, little one." One of the customers shifted slightly to look at me telling me in the restrained monotone of his greeting that I was both an unwelcome distraction and a novelty. How many teenage girls walked into a bar on a weekday afternoon? How many had ever seen a bar? Other men began to turn and look.

"What's up? What's she want?"

"Is my father here?"

"Who might that be?" the man who'd greeted me asked. Somebody laughed.

The bartender came forward into the light, brought his hand down on the bar and shushed the laughter. I was so glad to see him, a man named Bob Lively who had worked part-time at the old place, the home place. He always wore a stiff white shirt and a conservative tie, formal as if he were tending bar at Shangri-La.

"I'm looking for my father." I hoped my father would turn out to be around, in the cellar or just next door at the bakery.

"Were you supposed to meet him?" Lively asked carefully. "He didn't mention it." Lively had always seemed ready for me and my mother, the way he shepherded us to a back booth and poured a Coke and a Nehi Orange.

"I just thought maybe I could find him."

Lively rubbed his upper lip. The customers looked back and forth from him to me. Some of them gave him suggestions. "Give her a drink." "Sit down girl." "You need money to get home? Give her car fare."

Lively said, measuring me, "I think he's at the Bedford Hunting and Fishing Club." I looked blank, I'm sure. "You never been there, huh?"

"No."

"Know where it is?"

"No."

He nodded. Then he turned and swooped into the cooler to his right, behind the bar and low, out of sight, and he came up with a dripping bottle of Nehi Orange. He opened it on the side of the cooler. He took a glass from the sink where many stood, lined up on a towel, and poured the drink into the side of the glass as if he were pouring beer. "You go back there and sit down," he said. "I'll try to find him."

I did as I was told, my stomach twisting in nervousness, my purpose (a talk with my father) forgotten in the new problem of finding him. My books, which I piled high on the table, gave me a place to rest my head while I waited. I saw that Lively consulted a paper taped to the wall before he made a phone call from the pay phone at the end of the bar. The men watched him, and he gave me a sidelong glance while he spoke. When he finished, he looked at me directly. The men turned and looked at me, too.

Lively came to my table with a small white notepad and a pencil. "You know where Franklin Street is?" he asked. "You know where Market Street is?"

I nodded. "I just came from there."

He wrote down an address, which he said was "the club," and he told me to go down to the basement entrance and to press the button for the third floor. The door would open to me when the buzzer sounded. I was supposed to open it and walk up to the third floor. It reminded me of the song "Green Door," something sneaky.

"Can you find it?"

"Yes." A terrible disappointment came over me, a feeling of hopelessness. Why hadn't my father left whatever place he was in to come find me? Why hadn't he read my gesture as a call for help, something out of the ordinary? Heaviness came over me as I walked to the Bedford Hunting and Fishing Club.

This would be a new side of my father, I urged myself on, a hunting and fishing father. I imagined men sitting around in red plaid shirts and caps with bills, talking about guns and bait. Maybe gazing at displays on the walls. Examining maps, telling fish stories. Things my father never talked about at home.

But when I got there, when I made it through the basement entrance and up the four flights of stairs to the third floor, there wasn't a red shirt or a fishing rod in sight.

It was a bar. Just a bar. Bigger than either of my father's, I thought, and with more women customers, almost as many as men. And not just *one* pin ball machine in a corner but four or five of them and a whole row of other kinds, the most common of which I was to learn moments later was the one-armed bandit.

"What's up?" my father greeted me cheerfully. "Need a ride home?"

"Yes."

"Where's Mom?"

"I came alone."

"Shopping?"

"Sort of." I saw that we couldn't talk there. It was noisier than either of the two other bars I knew.

"Boy, you sure are grown up, huh?"

"Getting there."

My father took my hand and took me up to the bar. "Give her a Nehi Orange," he said. "And a roll of quarters."

"Yes, sir," the bartender said.

Then my father turned to a broad-faced, tightly permed woman and said, "Hey, Lillian, show my girl how to use the slot machines." He called to the bartender and asked for another roll of quarters, tapping the bar in front of Lillian. "Have a good time," he said to us.

Lillian didn't do so well at the machines. She swore and then apologized. I ended up with more quarters than I started with. "Beginner's luck," she said. "Always the way."

I carried my quarters in a pouch to the bar and after my father nodded to the bartender, they were replaced with a ten dollar bill and three ones. I tried to give it back to my father, but the gesture made all the men around him laugh. My father laughed, too. He told me it was mine to keep. I was amazed. It was a quarter of my mother's weekly allowance.

Finally we left.

"Dad," I said. "Dad. . . ."

He looked at me from his slightly bent-forward position as he put the key into the ignition. His movement was slow, almost mesmerizingly deliberate. "What, sweetheart?" The car motor started up and he looked from the ignition to the lever, which he moved to shift the car from park into drive.

"I came to town to talk to you."

There was a split second hesitation in him, a strengthening of himself for whatever he would have to do, before he said in a bright voice, a voice that showed the world was good and he could fix the parts that weren't so good, "What's up, sweetheart?"

"I want to talk to you about Mom."

"Oh?" And he needed a moment again to come fully to the conversation, maybe to fortify himself.

"It's Mom. She's angry all the time. She hits me."

"Does she?" he asked, but he knew it, as we all knew things about each other, as somewhere just out of reach of everyday consciousness we knew that he was involved in a part ownership of the illegal Bedford Hunting and Fishing Club. The secrecy and the complex nature of his proprietorship there was a marker for a segment of his life and ours, the chunk of time that naturally followed the home bar and the town bar, but was something altogether different, something that made him even more difficult to find and fetch. "Does she?"

The Pirates are winning. Harrison puts an arm around me and says, "You're far away. Thinking about dark things, eh?"

"Afraid so."

"Want a beer?"

"Okay."

The film is black and white, an art film, dark. I am at the hospital wearing the big green hat, except it has no color in the film-memory.

My sisters and I are in the sixth floor corner waiting room while two doors away my mother is in the room occupied by my father. I just arrived, an hour ago. My job in the time I've been here has been to track down my brother Andy where he tends bar in New Jersey. I still have a handful of change—a pocketful, too—left over from my efforts, which were finally successful. Although I was not able to speak to Andy myself, I explained the situation to his friend Joe, who will put him in a car and drive him here.

I wear a sundress and a large straw hat of an unusual shade of green, lime I suppose you'd call it, full of light. The hat came from a fashionable boutique in the East Village.

It is ten o'clock at night. I have finally taken off my sunglasses, but I will not take off my hat. It is special, wild, and conveys cheer. Men on the street, strangers, compliment me on it. One handsome man said, "Wonderful hat!" and tipped an invisible one to me. I want my father to be amused by it—and me. I want to make him laugh.

My sisters and my mother and I say odd, unimportant things to each other. "Does your back still hurt?" "Would you like another cup of coffee?"

I wear my hat and stride from corner to corner, pouring cups of coffee. As long as I wear the hat, I won't cry. Inside from my abdomen to my chest everything is tight and in pain.

Nobody asks me any questions about my life. This is just as well because I can't tell them about my disastrous affair, now ended, with a man older than me, harsh and way out of my league. I would like to lie down somewhere. I would like to die. But the truth is, I'm going to be alive for a long time yet. I'm wearing a huge green hat to symbolize it. My father is dying. That's what's happening. He wants to see me, my mother assures me, but he keeps asking about my brother, she says. He is hanging on for that.

The boy who walks into the waiting room where we sit on rose-colored plastic couches is not my brother but Eddie Petrosky, my brother's age, an acquaintance of my brother's, a boy my father almost killed once when he was driving the

Oldsmobile up Howard's Hill and Eddie was riding a bike. Eddie is wearing a khaki shirt and darker khaki pants, which even though they don't match look like a military uniform.

"I'm going into the army in three months," he tells us. "I feel I should." He will go to Viet Nam and be killed, shot out of a tree, broken open, his guts spilling all over foreign ground. At his funeral his family will say that he loved my father and that my father made a difference in those ten years of life between the ages of nine and nineteen. That will seem credible to those of us who were primed to hear of the curative powers of my father's presence. What he did for Eddie became part of the family legend.

"Ah, it's going to be one of those off-nights," Harrison says. The Pirates have gotten behind. "Listen. When this is over, don't go home. Come to my place. Stay overnight. I'll wake you early. You can go home in the morning." His car is still downtown at the newspaper office where we both work.

"I'm writing a major story."

"Oh. You can have a good night's sleep at my place," he offers brightly. "You could tell me what you're thinking."

His arm is around me, the hug it promises is too good to miss. "I'll come over."

"Good!"

I put down my almost full container of beer. It's warm and flat, bitter.

My father is coming down Beatrice, and he stops at the corner, but not completely—nobody does. He steers the Oldsmobile awkwardly around the turn and starts up Howard Hill, not all that fast, because it's steep and the Olds is automatic and can only do what it is programmed for, given a start from the bottom of a hill. Howard's Hill is steep enough to be *really* good in wintertime for sled-riding. On this particular day, it happens to be early spring, but the sky is winterish in appearance. Out of the alley to the right comes Eddie Petrosky on his bike. To my father he is a phantom who appears out of nowhere, a mote in the mind's eye. My father swerves—a beat late?—but hits him anyway. He feels—I imagine, even though it isn't possible, that he *feels*—the Olds make contact with both the bike and the body of the boy. Eddie flies a little distance before he falls. At just the interval in which Eddie goes through the air, making his arc, his parents, who have been sitting on their dilapidated corner porch just next to the alley, stand. Their stand and Eddie's flight are exactly coordinated.

My father stops the car in the middle of the hill and steps carefully on the emergency brake. He is shaking so that he can hardly walk. Yet, somehow, he gets to Eddie before Eddie's parents do. Kneeling down on the blacktop of Howard's Hill, my father says, "Hey, fella, all right? Had a spill, eh?" Eddie's eyes try to close, but he breathes in the smell of my father, Old Spice, cigarettes, whiskey, and it is like a potion that revives him. He says, "Uh huh."

Perhaps in reality Eddie was already scrambling up to see if his bicycle was wrecked. Or maybe he yelled and whimpered *oowwww* as children do who are weak in spirit, ready for blows. But as I see it when I call up the scene, Eddie lies there, a pale and frightened waif of nine, looking up at my father and giving up all his life to him. (Surely my father had heard that one should never move an accident victim, but in those moments he paid no attention to once-heard warnings.) He gathers the boy in his arms, saying, "You're going to be all right, you're going to be fine." Then he tells Eddie's parents, "Get into the car . We'll take him to the hospital." They say, "No," and look at each other because they are frightened about the cost. But my father nods at them, a gentle order, and they go to open the door for him, they climb into the Olds, Mr. Petrosky up front with my father, Mrs. Petrosky in the backseat with Eddie. My father drives carefully-fast to Lee Hospital, looking back over his shoulder whenever they are stopped at red lights to ask Eddie, "New bike?" "Riding long?" To anything Eddie mumbles, he says, "That's the sport. That's right, kiddo."

My father finally arrived home, even later than usual.

The accident with Eddie happened during the Bedford Hunting and Fishing Club days. My mother was still trying to turn things backwards to when they were sweeter, to how they used to be when I was six and Genevieve was four and Andy a baby of one. My father used to come home earlier then, in the old Elias Grill days. He would sit in the rocking chair in the sun parlor and hold us, all three of us on him somehow, and he would rock and sing. There must have been rainy days, sometimes, but I remember the sun always shining low through the panes of glass.

"Two hundred and sixty-two panes of glass," my mother would say happily, having cleaned and shined them all. She wore sundresses with ruffly shoulder straps then, and she tied her hair back and had a pompadour in front. She would stand in the archway of the sun parlor and watch us climbing all over my father, and the picture seemed to make her happy.

He sang, "*I want a girl just like the girl that married dear old Dad,*" and also, "*There was a big fat lady, a-standing on the streetcar track. And when the streetcar came, she ran from front to back.*" I was very literal at six. I could see the fat lady, an omnibus of a woman, on the tracks right outside the bar and all the customers gathered around my father to find out what he thought as the conductor tried to get her in. I thought, too, that when my father sang, "*I want a girl,*" not that he was trying to order a perfect wife but that he was ordering a perfect daughter who would be just like the perfect wife who married dear old Dad. My mother would re-enter the sun parlor with a spatula in her hand, between flips of whatever she was making for supper. She would laugh and bask as much as any of us did, and I determined to be like her, "*a good old-fashioned girl with heart so true, one who loved nobody else but you.*"

"*Your father. What sort of man was he?*"

"*. . .a big man. A Santa Claus of a man. Always the promise of something wonderful. We were always waiting for him.*"

The game is over and we have left Harrison's car downtown. We enter Harrison's house and go straight to the kitchen. He routs around in the refrigerator for an after-the-game treat and finds spaghetti and marinara sauce.

"*In the early days, he would come home from work and sit in the rocking chair in the sun parlor and hold us. There were three of us then—somehow he could hold all three of us on him—and he would rock and sing. The sun would be shining right on us, low, through the panes of glass. It was wonderful."*

He pours us each a glass of wine and toasts, "Here's to your father, to Andrew."

On the night that my father hit Eddie Petrosky I'd already set the table and dressed the salad, as usual. And as usual, I sat on the red stool and studied my mother. I often hung around her, bound to her, identified with her. At six-thirty, she put the yellow casserole dish, which contained round steak and gravy, back into the oven and said to me, "Helen, call town and, if he's not there, the grill." She was still desperately in love with my father and didn't like to do anything that might ruffle things between them.

In the living room, Andy, nine, was pulling Pamela's hair and pressing her fingers back until she screamed. She was five then and getting used to it. She'd pretty much missed the rocking and singing phase in the sun parlor. I poked my head into the dining room where Genevieve, twelve (but it might have been any time in her life, the way she was fixed, poised over the table, laboriously tracing the holes of the lace table cloth) suffered over her homework. I moved from room to room like a pencil following the dots. "Stop that!" I told Andy. He laughed at me and motioned to Pamela to be quiet while I was on the phone. Then he pinched her, a long sustained pinch, while he told her to keep her scream silent. They were as used to these routines as I was to being my mother's right hand.

When I called any of the places, somebody—usually Lively or Chick or Solo, the bartenders—would say, "He's just left."

"When my father arrived home we would run at him with hugs and kisses and hang on him so desperately that he couldn't even walk to the big chair, his recliner. He would tell my mother, 'I got tied up.'

"Something about that expression—maybe it was just that Andy and Pamela were usually surfacing from a cowboy program of some sort— made me picture a bunch of guys tying

my father to a post. But he was the hero, not the villain, he was the Gary Cooper, not the man in black. They tied him up because they couldn't get enough of him. Nobody could get enough of him. I never could."

Harrison shakes his head sympathetically as he takes out separate pots to heat everything.

And then, after that spring day, there had to be a piece of him, too, for Eddie Petrosky, who from that night on for a little more than ten years engaged in the life of our family.

When we heard the Oldsmobile purr and shut off, we always dropped whatever we'd been doing and gathered before the door in the living room. The car door would slam. My mother would open the front door, my father would hug her, sometimes even lift her in the air. In this decade she wore dirndl skirts and cotton blouses, plaid or with little prints, very clean and sporty, and she tied her hair back with a ribbon. She called to mind a little girl advertising Ivory soap. She would kiss my father on the cheek and take off his fedora, which he wore every day with a zip-up cotton windbreaker. "Handsome!" she'd say. She would ask him how he was as she unzipped his jacket, and then she would hand these bits of clothing back to me and Genevieve, who put them in the hall closet while we waited our turn to be noticed.

On normal days he would sit in the big chair, and she would remove his shoes, then pull his socks away from his feet so they didn't stick. That was a job I wanted. I fought for it and after a while I got it. My mother would say, "Okay, you can do his socks."

But of course on this day, there were no foot rituals, nor did he say the usual line about being tied up. "I hit a kid," he said. "He was on his bike."

We stopped in the midst of our moves.

"I just came from the hospital. They think it's a concussion, and they're checking for internal bleeding. He's pale as the dickens, so I think he's bleeding. I'm going to go back when dinner's over and they know something."

"You poor thing," my mother said, holding on to him. "Why do you have to go?"

"I want to," he said. We looked at him with awe because he chose to go. "Eddie Petrosky is the boy's name," he told us. "Do you know him?"

I didn't. Genevieve didn't. But Andy said, "*Oh! Eddie!*"

"Why do you say it that way?" I asked.

"He's a goon. No one will play with him."

"What do you mean, 'a goon?'" my mother asked eagerly.

"He's dumb. He always falls asleep in school," Andy snorted.

"He couldn't get out of the way fast enough," my mother guessed. With more certainty, she shook her head and said quietly, "A slow kind of kid. And you drove them all to the hospital!" While round steak and gravy waited, I suppose she meant.

My father's hands shook, and I saw, as I sat across from him at dinner, that he was not eating his round steak. Years later we would watch him not eating, meal after meal, day after day. I would not be able to stand it, and I would run away.

The night he hit Eddie, I saw he was frightened. I knew that he was full of alcohol, although this was not something I thought of as necessarily bad. It was part of his magic—the slow mesmerizing way he moved, the dreaminess, the smile he summoned as he brought his atmosphere into focus. The magic of spirits, along with his black hair and blue eyes, made him an adult, large, steady-seeming version of Ricky Nelson, Elvis, and my current preoccupation, Bobby Darlenz, who lived down on Beatrice Avenue and whom I searched for every day. I said, "Do you have to go to the hospital?"

"Yes," he said. "Gotta go."

Drying dishes, I asked my mother, who washed, "Do you think the accident was Dad's fault?"

"You heard yourself the kid was a slow kid," she said. "Maybe his family doesn't eat enough meat," she mused. "Some people don't. Some people, you know, eat noodles, vegetables, bread, and that's it! Can you imagine?"

We ate meat, we had an immaculate kitchen, we had something fresh to wear to school every day. We were not slow. And certainly my father was not at fault.

"When I was a teenager," my mother told me, "some of the girls would throw themselves in front of cars all the time. Millie Salinas used to do it every two years or so. That's how she bought her school clothes. And the rest of her family's clothes, too."

"I don't get it."

"Insurance."

"But didn't she get hurt?"

"Sure. She flew a couple of times. She'd get banged up pretty good. Otherwise she wouldn't have been able to collect."

I sat on the red stool, stalled in my work.

"Get moving," she said. "There's the breakfast room to clean up and homework to do."

"But she might have been killed."

"Oh, she knew how to get hit," she said.

"People used to say there was something about my father that was—I don't know—life giving."

"Even better than Santa Claus." Harrison has just *unearthed the littlest bit of chocolate almond ice cream from the freezer. I open two drawers and find things, all kinds of things from hardware to tooth picks. In the third drawer, I find spoons. "Hooray. Spoons."*

Eddie Petrosky not only lived but thrived. Reports began to come in, some given straight to my mother, who identified herself to Mary Petrosky at Balya's store as Andrew Elias's wife; some through Andy, who saw Eddie at school; some through my father, who now saw Mr. Petrosky at the bar every once in a while. The word was that Eddie got smart after my father hit him, that he became a different child after that, quicker, more intelligent. He stayed awake in school, his hair grew thicker, and he put on weight. My mother even reported that she'd seen him with Mary Petrosky at Balya's one day and that he had cheek-roses and was eyeing up the candy.

There were theories about this transformation in Eddie. His family believed that before the accident he felt puny and negligible, but afterwards, he felt important. It hadn't happened to anyone else he knew. Andy thought it was the baseball mitt and the bat and the new bike my father took to the hospital for him. My mother said the blow itself was good for him. "It kind of *knocked* something into him." But I thought then, and think still, that it was my father's hospital visits—all day, every day, for two weeks—that changed Eddie's life.

Eddie began to stop for Andy on the way to school. And pretty soon they were friends.

One day on the way down Howard Hill to Beatrice Avenue to look for Bobby Darlenz, who sometimes didn't answer me when I said hello and who sometimes could be heard laughing with his friends after I passed his house, I saw Eddie making fast circles and figure eights with his new bike, his new cap pushed way back on his head as only the confident dare wear their caps. He was cured of defeat. I looked at him with envy.

"My father had patience with hospitals, illnesses." I have already told Harrison about this thing I had, what the doctor called a grapefruit-sized growth sitting on my ovary. "Remember my scar?" Harrison nods respectfully. "He sat on a metal chair in the hospital room day after day, just sitting with me. I don't know where he ever found the patience. But he just sat there until I started to feel better."

I can see that Harrison, putting aside his ice cream, is about to say something kind and sentimental, but this is not what I want, not what I mean.

"Once he hit a boy on a bike, but the boy forgave him, even came to love him."

"Oh?"

"I'd like to see him," Eddie says. He is six feet tall, slim but well-built; his brown hair is thick. He has wide Slavic cheekbones, which get patches of red when he asks to see my father. "Me and him got to be buddies."

"How did you know he was in the hospital again?" I asked.

"My girlfriend works in admissions. After the first couple of times, I told her to keep me posted."

"They're only allowing family," Genevieve says.

Eddie looks at her, and although he smiles at her, I think he sees that she is the classic, tough, small, delicate, soft-spoken person you don't want to argue with. She looks away from him and slightly downwards, her archetypal position, as if she is forever laboring over equations or wars at the dining room table, tracing the lace pattern of the table cloth, poking the pencil eraser through the holes in the lace, while she forces herself to go back to doing sums.

"Hi, Eddie!" Pamela says to distract him. "It's me. Remember? Come sit over here. How have you been? You're joining the army in three months! When did you decide?"

For a moment Eddie forgets his mission.

My mother comes out of the room in which my father lies and nods to me. I am next. I have not seen him since I arrived at the Pittsburgh hospital, and Genevieve and Pamela have seen him many times today.

Before I go in, I see my mother register Eddie's presence. I stop for a moment to squeeze her hand. These days she wears polyester pants suits with nylon blouses. Her hair is cut into a puffy short style and has as much salt as pepper.

Harrison puts the chocolaty dishes in the sink without rinsing them.

"We avoided him when he was dying. Until the end. I got there at the end, but I couldn't really talk to him. . . .I still blame myself for not being there."

I can see the skeleton under my father, the small assemblage of bones that gives him form. I can see what he is about to become. He is like a spirit—the skin stretched over his bones is iridescent. His eyes are closed.

I see that the metal-legged chair that is near the bed will make noise if I move it, so I sit in it just where it is, at an odd angle to the bed, and wait for him to waken to me. Half-turned away like this and waiting is *my* perpetual position, archetypal, my version of homework at the lace table cloth. I sit quietly without comfort at an odd angle. I want to ask him all the important questions, even the ones he has already answered, but somehow I don't get to.

I wait for a long time.

A nurse comes in and like a *grande dame* of the thirties at her bellpull, jiggles my father's IV tube and walks out. He opens his eyes. I make a face like, "Here I am, suntanned, and wild, and wearing a crazy hat."

"Where did you get that?" He tries to gesture toward my big hat and he laughs dutifully.

"New York! Pretty fancy, huh?"

His lips move as if he is saying, "Pretty fancy," but he doesn't produce any sound. His mouth looks uncomfortably dry.

"Let me get you water," I say. "We have to keep up your strength."

"Is Andy *here*?" my father asks as if I've just said he is.

"No." I want Andy's time so long as he's not here. "Want me to tell you about New York?" I ask.

Just then, the same grand nurse who woke him enters like an omnibus and says, "Mr. Elias. I've got a special request. There's a young man out there, says he's *almost* family, name is Eddie Petrosky, and he wants to see you."

I shake my head no, grasping at my limited time here, all the things I want to ask, all the things I want to say. I explain and I embroider: "Eddie's girlfriend works in admissions. That's how he knew you were in here. We've kept it quiet. Otherwise you'd have a line of guys out there keeping you awake all night." The truth is, they've abandoned him. My mother said they left him in proportion to his weight loss as if they were bits and pieces of him, the fabric of his largeness.

I hear my father say, "All right. Send him in."

Moments later, Eddie comes into the room. Framed in the doorway, in his khakis, in the light of nighttime, he looks absolutely handsome. As I leave them to each other, I hear my father give a weakened, "Eddie! Hey! How's it going?" Surely Eddie can hear it's only a shadow of a greeting. Surely Eddie will not overstay, and I, interrupted, will have another turn. But all of this is wrong. An hour later he is gone and I have had no more time with him and am left still wishing for it.

Out in the waiting room, after the fact, at two in the morning, my mother tells us what happened: She got tired of waiting and went into my father's room. Eddie was just sitting there, talking about going to Viet Nam and about the girlfriend he was leaving behind. Before my mother could say anything to Eddie, an intern, someone she'd never seen before, came into the room and pushed right in front of her.

The intern said, jovially, as if this were a party, "Mind if I have a look?"

And Eddie, who had no business answering, said, "Sure, I'll get out of your way." Eddie stepped aside and sort of offered my father, but still he didn't get out of the room.

"Your pancreas, eh?" the intern asked consulting a chart. "Nasty thing, huh? Just let me have a feel!"

And then, according to my mother, the intern stood over my father and pressed down on his upper belly, hard. My mother heard a crackle, like newspaper, and then she heard something break.

My father let out a groan of pain and said, "Oh, no." Then he gave a long look straight to my mother and shook his head. The intern backed out of the room.

"Is Andy here?" my father asked.

"On his way," she said. But she knew it was too late.

"I'm here," Eddie said. "Mr. Elias? I'm still here."

"When the doctor pressed, something broke," my mother told us. "Something went out of him." There was nothing, she meant, but a thin membrane between life and death, something as dry and crackly as old newspaper. Thin as the year Eddie had left before his outer layer broke open and let him out, too. Thin and fragile as the next twenty years, which went by like a breath.

I am about to tell Harrison the surprising feeling that has welled up in me. I am about to say, "Sometimes I hate him." It's an awful feeling.

But Harrison has a finger to his lips. Even though he isn't looking at me, I fall silent. Moments later we turn out the lights and start up the stairs. "Did you know that he loved you?" he asks.

"I guess I never doubted it."

"And you adored him. It sounds like. Didn't you?" The man asks a lot of questions.

"We all did."

He turns out more lights and runs a hand up and down my back as we climb the last flight of stairs. My chest is tight. Can he feel that I am about to cry?

"You adored him?"

"Totally."

"I would have liked him, I'm sure."

No chitchat here. No, there is no question at all where we are going or that we are going. Things progress, and that's the miracle of it, in a word.